Insurrection, Book 1

Rise of the Revolution

C. J. Korryn

Published by C. J. Korryn Books 2020

Published by:

C. J. Korryn Books

✱✱✱✱

©2020 by C. J. Korryn

✱✱✱✱

Visit C. J. Korryn's website for more of his books.

https://www.cjkorryn.com/books

Check out the monthly installments of season two and later seasons.

https://www.cjkorrynserialsubscriptions.com/

1

Aurik Shulz shivered awake, the air hitting his wet skin with a biting force. He brought his arms up to his chest in a futile effort to warm himself.

The air itself wasn't cold, but the watery fluid that covered his entire body was. When the air collided with it, it seemed to get even colder.

He knew the cold sensation would pass shortly, just like his blurry vision, when his body adjusted to being out of suspended animation. He had to adjust from months of being in stasis. His eyes began to focus, and though he was still cold, it didn't seem as severe as before.

He noticed, when his eyes finally focused, that the room he was in wasn't the stasis pod room that he and his counterparts were supposed to wake up in. The room was large and white, and there was a window on the far wall. It was dark beyond the window, but he felt that someone was watching him.

He immediately knew something was wrong. The stasis pod room contained no windows and was not white. He stepped out of his pod, bringing a fresh sensation of cold as he moved through the air. He was almost naked, wearing only underwear. It was soaked through, itself, which did not allow for any reprieve from the cold currents of air. As Aurik moved, even his undergarment seemed like it was soaked in ice water as it clung to him.

He still wasn't fully recovered from stasis, and as he stepped out of the pod he stumbled, more than walked, to the large window. He leaned his hands against it to steady himself as he looked around the room.

He saw four more pods, the rest of his squad, with the doors open. They were beginning to stir. He heard one of his crew gasp awake, then another, and finally the last two. He walked over to the closest.

"Sarah," he said with a heavy German accent as she started glancing around.

"Where are we?" She asked.

"I don't know, but we are not on our ship," he replied.

Sarah's long soaked wet hair even darker than its usual deep brown that matched her eyes. She was dark-complected, contrasting with Aurik's pale skin.

"Aurik, what's going on?" Came a deep Texas twang from across the room. Aurik peered around Sarah's stasis pod to see the rest of his squad carefully stepping out of their pods.

The one who spoke, Kyle Jackson, was a burly built man with short, brown hair. Next to him was Jessica, an African American, whose long, straight black hair, weighed down from being wet, clung to her ebony skin. Next to her was a Chinese woman with hair that hung heavily down to her jaw and bangs that fell to just above her eyes, framing her face, Yin Shou. They all wore black undergarments soaked through with the water like stasis liquid.

"Where are we? Yin asked.

"I don't know. I don't know what happened," Aurik replied.

The window suddenly illuminated, revealing an observation room with half a dozen N'Roth staring at them. The squad each stared in shock at the creatures that held them captive.

The N'Roth were humanoid in appearance. However, that was about where the similarities ended. There was no mistaking them for humans. The N'Roth were genderless and hairless with pink eyes. Their hands and feet – if you could call them that – had three digits that looked more like fleshy pinchers than toes or fingers. Their skin was pale with an icy blue tint that gave them a look of a dead, lifeless human. They had thick, black, scaly veins that ran along their bodies, and made them look like a decayed, cracked, dry, desert lake bed. Instead of ears, they had bumpy scales with several slits in them. Instead of a nose, an indention with several slits.

Like humans, though, they wore clothing. The half dozen in the observation room wore brown, form-fitting garments that clung to their bodies. On the center of their chests was an insignia of some sort.

The crew of five stared back at the half-dozen alien creatures observing them. Moments later, a large door to the left of the observation room slid open, and a half dozen armed N'Roth rushed into the room.

The squad stepped back as the N'Roth raised their weapons toward them.

"Follow the soldiers to your cells," came a scratchy voice from the intercom. One of the soldiers motioned with his gun for the squad to move.

The weapon was unlike anything they had ever seen before. It looked to be a rifle of some sort. Its buttstock rested under the armpit of its wielder curving upward around the inside of the arm until it rested against the forearm of its user allowing for a snug fit against the wielder's forearm. At elbow length, protruded a grip of three to four inches long, which the wielder held with his off-hand, securing it tightly in its pinchers. A few inches farther, the muzzle widened into an oval-shape with a trigger on the underside of the weapon and a notch on top into which the N'Roth pinchers rested.

Aurik obeyed, knowing that the only other options were to disobey and likely be shot on the spot or to fight their way out, and they were ill-equipped to fight their way out.

The rest of his squad followed suit. The warm metal flooring slippery under their wet, dripping bodies.

Aurik noticed that the corridors were massive, more than enough room for a row of three. The doors, as well, were oversized, and the ceiling was much higher than the N'Roth needed them to be. He could tell that it was a massive facility. He was taking note of everything he could remember. The soldier's weapons, how they moved, the doors, the corridors they passed by, the N'Roth who stared as they walked by. He tried to be discreet as he glanced around and hoped the N'Roth did not notice him peering into each room as they passed by open doors. He noticed several maintenance hatches, again

oversized, as well.

Though the corridors were clear of any consoles, it

seemed the rooms he peered into had consoles and

workstations, and he counted the steps at each turn, each door,

each passing corridor, trying his best to memorize his steps and

turns.

He knew the rest of his team were similarly already

plotting their escape, though, in truth, he had no idea how they

were going to get out of this mess – whatever mess it was that

they were in. He had no idea – yet. If there was anyone who

could find a way out of this, it was his team. They were the

best of the best. That was why they were put together.

They were finally led into the brig and separated into

two cells, the men in one, the women in the other. The second

they were in the cells, they heard the buzz of power. The cell

entryway lit up, and what looked like tiny bolts of lightning

bounced back and forth along the entryway threshold.

"Well, at least the N'Roth like it warm," Jessica said. The rest of the squad either ignored her or smiled in response, their conundrum weighing heavily on them.

"What is going on, Aurik? How did we get here?" Sarah asked.

Aurik shook his head.

"I don't know. I woke up right before the rest of you," he replied.

"One thing's for sure. We have to get out of here, wherever here is. Jessica, you think you can figure this security system out?"

Jessica glanced around her cell and investigated the entryway. "I will do the best I can." Aurik nodded and started studying the cell himself.

Kyle, who had already been examining the cell, was fixated on the miniature lightning bouncing around the entryway.

"Have you ever seen anything like this?" He asked Aurik.

"No," Aurik replied, "But I wouldn't want to -" Aurik's reply was cut short by a sudden, loud crackling, pop, and thud. He spun around to see Kyle unconscious, leaning against the back wall. He rushed over to him, immediately realizing what Kyle had done. He pressed two fingers to Kyle's neck and felt a shockingly strong pulse.

Kyle suddenly lurched forward with a gasp, startling Aurik, who fell backward.

"That was a stupid idea," Kyle said more to himself than Aurik. "I hurt all over." He stood to his feet, cringing, his heart pounding.

"You are so stupid!" Yin angrily hollered, her Chinese accent heavy. "You should know not to touch that!"

Jessica smiled at Yin's outburst. Though Yin wouldn't admit it, she had feelings for Kyle, and Jessica knew that was why she was so angry. Kyle shrugged as he slowly stood to his feet, every inch of him in pain.

"Well, at least we know what that force field does," Aurik said.

Jessica started feeling along the frame of the force field, being careful not to touch the field itself. She felt an edge right before the energy barrier, assuming it to be the frame for the force field itself. She thought it as good a place as any to try and find a way to turn it off. She closed her eyes as she ran her hands along this edge, feeling for anything, for bumps, scratches, dents, screws, anything that might give her a clue about the wiring or mechanics of the force field. She ran her hands down one side of the entryway frame, then started along the opposite side, going up until she came to her starting point at the top, taking particular notice of each imperfection.

After she finished with the entryway frame, she started feeling the flooring. She noticed in the corner nearest the wall, a slight temperature difference. Upon closer inspection, she felt and saw tiny slits where the entry frame met the floor.

"I found something. The floor is slightly warmer here, and there are four slits in this corner. It might be something like screws," she informed the others.

"Better than nothing," Aurik replied.

The door at the main entrance to the brig hissed open, and five N'Roth entered. Two walked over to Kyle and Aurik's cell, two walked over to the women's cell, and the last one stayed near the door, its weapon at the ready.

The two at each cell raised what looked like weapons at the entryway and turned the force field off. The devices looked similar to the rifles they saw earlier. The barrels were wide and oval-shaped with a grip behind the barrels on which the N'Roth's pinchers rested naturally.

Each pair selected one of their corresponding cell occupants with a wave of their pistols, ordering them to step out of the cells. Aurik and Sarah stepped out as ordered and cooperated with every demand as the N'Roth soldiers escorted them out of the brig. The soldiers escorted the two down several corridors, then the two N'Roth escorting Sarah veered off down an adjacent corridor.

A few moments later, Aurik found himself back in the room with the stasis pods. An N'Roth stood among the pods, peering into the back panel of one.

"Ah, Aurik, is it?" The N'Roth asked in a familiar, scratchy voice. "That is what the female called you,"

"You were the one who spoke through the intercom earlier."

"No. We all seem to sound the same to you humans," he explained.

"Why were you in these stasis pods?" It asked. "This is remarkable understanding of technology for humans. How did you make it?"

Aurik could sense the hostility in its scratchy voice, despite the calm, friendly tone in which it spoke.

Aurik didn't answer.

The N'Roth interrogator had been admiring the mechanics of the stasis unit more than paying attention to Aurik looked up when he didn't answer.

The two locked gazes, the N'Roth sensing the defiance in Aurik and Aurik noticing the cold, heartless, and ruthlessness behind the N'Roth's pink eyes.

The N'Roth stalked over to him, an aura of rage emanating from it, a scowl on its face and its black, scaly veins pulsing in fury.

***

Sarah was left alone in a large room. No soldiers, no forcefields, no security. She glanced around the room, noticing a couch on the far wall and a cocktail bar on the adjoining wall. There was also a large table in the center of the room that held a bowl of apples, grapes, mangos, oranges, and several other alien fruits she didn't recognize. She thought it curious how human everything looked.

The door behind her hissed open, and she turned around.

"Please, take a seat, have some fruit, relax," The N'Roth said in its scratchy voice as it walked past her, seeming almost to ignore her.

She followed the alien with her eyes, unsure of what to make of the situation. The N'Roth's countenance seemed that of a friend and not of an enemy, and its voice, though scratchy and forced as it was, was kind.

She watched it rummage through the fruit bowl and snatch up two. One was blue in color, squiggly, long and scaly. Its shape resembled two S's put together. The other was an orange. He walked over to her and offered her both fruits.

"Do they have Zeret on the planet you are from?" He asked. Sarah didn't reply. The N'Roth smiled and walked back over to the table.

"I understand why you don't trust us. Whatever planet you come from, they probably told you we are evil." It sat down on the couch.

"What is your name?" He asked.

She didn't answer.

He smiled.

"Very well," it replied, crossing its legs.

"Let me be honest with you." The N'Roth's demeanor suddenly changed. Its face grew stern, its body, more rigid, and its voice harsh. "We will find out everything we need to know. It is better for you and your friends if you tell us now." It stood up, seeming to change personalities again.

"Do you want a drink? I have grown fond of your human drinks," it said as it walked over to the bar.

"You know, we have a team of scientists going through your ship right now." The alien grabbed a glass and poured itself a drink. "It is quite old. We are curious as to where you found it." It took a sip as it glared at Sarah, noticing the confusion on her face. The N'Roth set the glass down.

"You have no idea what I'm talking about, do you?" It remarked, surprised. "Who are you, and where were you going in that old earth ship?" It asked, its scratchy voice suddenly ice cold, sending a shiver down Sarah's spine.

2

Aurik went rigid as the N'Roth bounded over to him. He knew there was nothing he could do. He was unarmed and knew that if he tried to defend himself that he would not leave the room alive, so he prepared himself for whatever was going to come.

The N'Roth never slowed as he neared, Aurik sensing the primal rage emanating from the alien. The N'Roth didn't skip a beat as it came nose to nose with Aurik, grabbing a handful of hair and yanking Aurik's head back.

"Where was your ship headed to!?" It yelled in fury. "How did you acquire such technology!?" It yanked hard on Aurik's hair, bringing a cringe to his face.

Aurik knew he had to say something, but didn't know what to say. He could not reveal their mission. They would all surely be dead if the N'Roth found out what their mission was.

"We were on a mining mission," Aurik lied. The N'Roth loosened its grip slightly.

"From what planet?"

"What do you mean?" The N'Roth yanked back on Aurik's head again.

"What planet!?" It screamed.

Aurik didn't know what to say. What did it mean 'what planet?' Humans came from only one planet.

"Earth," Aurik replied, saying the only habitable planet he could think of that made sense. There were only two or three planets suitable for human life, but none of them were colonized yet.

Again, the N'Roth loosened its grip.

"Earth has no mining facilities or ships."

Aurik had to think of something quickly.

"It was our first time. We were supposed to stay in stasis until we got near the planet to land."

The N'Roth released his hair and took a few steps away.

"If you were simply on a mining mission, where are the N'Roth commanders, and why do you have an arsenal of human weapons?"

Again, Aurik didn't know what the alien was talking about. The N'Roth turned slowly towards Aurik. He knew he had better say something.

"I don't know about the commanders, but our weapons were for protection against wild beasts." The N'Roth starred at him.

"Hm," it replied.

"All I know is that we went into the stasis pods on that ship, and we awoke here."

"So you claim," the N'Roth said coldly as it turned away, walking toward the stasis pods. "We have a team going through your ship, and we will find out everything we need to know," It turned back toward Aurik and said with an icy stare. "if you are lying, you will die." The N'Roth nodded to one of the two soldiers standing behind Aurik, who grabbed him by the arm.

"This way," it ordered.

***

The N'Roth stared at Sarah, his pink eyes drilling into her.

"Tell me what I want to know, and I can help you," it said, at last, its voice back to a friendly tone. It took one last gulp of his drink and casually walked towards Sarah. "You are only making things worse for you and your friends," it explained. "Give me something, anything, and I can help you." It stopped a few feet from her. "I can't help you unless you help me."

"You want me to give you something? Okay, I'll give you something." She lunged at the N'Roth, catching it off guard, and brought her elbow into the side of its face. The alien stumbled backward as Sarah kicked at its leg. It recovered in time to bring its leg up to block Sarah's kick and backhanded her. She went stumbling toward the table with the fruit bowl.

The N'Roth, infuriated by her sudden attack, charged at her. Sarah quickly found her footing and spun, sliding her hand across the fruit table, just in time to dodge its attack be dropping to the floor. It quickly turned as Sarah backed away on the floor. The alien came at her fast and angry, not noticing the object in her hand; faster than she anticipated. It grabbed her by the foot before she could get far enough away to get to her feet.

It dragged her closer to itself, and she kicked it in the face, ignoring the wave of pain as her bare foot contacted its face. If it had been a human, she would have broken its nose, but she had no idea what kicking an N'Roth in the face would do, as their noses were indentions rather than a human nose. It didn't seem to do much, other than cause the alien pain.

The N'Roth brought its hands up to its face as it stumbled backward.

Sarah jumped to her feet as quickly as she could and darted behind the bar. She grabbed a bottle and smashed it on the corner of the table, sending alcohol sprawling all over the floor and counter.

The N'Roth recovered from the kick in the face and again advanced. This time, it advanced with caution, realizing Sarah was not an ordinary woman. She had more spirit in her than any other human female he had encountered before.

She rushed at him with her arm out wide, bringing the jagged bottle down toward her opponent. She had no intention of killing him or even winning the fight. She had already accomplished what she had set out to do. She just needed to give the N'Roth a way to get the upper hand without making it obvious that she had let it win. The N'Roth saw its opening and brought its forearm up to block the wide swing as it stepped into Sarah's attack, bringing its other forearm up across her neck. The alien shoved with all its might, sending her stumbling backward into the wall, forced her arm out as far as it could until her hand hit the adjacent wall.

Sarah screamed at the sudden pain from her hand slamming into the wall and dropped her weapon. The N'Roth held its forearm at her throat, pressing in until Sarah lifted her hands in defeat. Despite her act of surrender and the sounds of her choking, it pressed in for a few more seconds, fueled by rage. Finally, the alien released her and spun her around, throwing her hard against the wall. It quickly grabbed both of her hands and forced them around, high on her back until she screamed in pain again, its pinchers digging into her hands as it held her tight. Without a word, the N'Roth pulled her backward, hard, directing her by yanking on her arms. It roughly shoved her to the door and handed her off to the two soldiers who had escorted her from the brig.

"Take her back to her cell. If she struggles, kill her," it told the soldiers. They nodded and escorted her back to the brig.

***

The door to the brig hissed open, and the two soldiers pushed Sarah into the room. Aurik and the others immediately noticed the bruise on Sarah's face. They all stared in concern and anger as the two soldiers released the force field, shoved Sarah into the cell, and re-instated the force field.

"Are you okay?" Aurik asked when the soldiers left.

"I'm fine," Sarah replied as she pulled a small paring knife from her underwear.

"I noticed this in the room where I was being interrogated. The only way I could think of to get it without being noticed was to lose a fight," she said with a smile. She handed the paring knife to Jessica.

"Will this help with those crevices you were talking about earlier?"

"It might." Jessica smiled.

"Well, we need to find a way out fast. The N'Roth are going through our ship as we speak, and when they find the mission files we are dead," Aurik reported.

"Understood," Jessica replied and immediately went to working on the cracks with the paring knife.

It wasn't long before Jessica successfully manipulated the three slits with the paring knife. It had been slow at first, but after she figured out how the crevices worked, it went quickly. She saw that the long cracks in the floor passed under the threshold of the force field. She hadn't noticed before because of the constant bouncing "lightning bolts" impairing her vision beyond the field. She had prodded inside the three openings, for which the paring knife was just small enough. She found that the middle slit felt slightly larger than the outside two, so she began working the knife in the center slot, surmising it to be the lock or latch. She had finally loosened the openings, which, in turn, enlarged the outside two, which she now saw ran several inches past the force field. After closer inspection, she realized the force field itself stopped about an inch from the floor.

Aurik and Kyle waited and watched, unable to see clearly through the force fields; but they knew not to disturb Jessica as she worked. Yin and Sarah, though they had a much better view of her progress, also knew not to distract her. They all stood quietly watching.

Jessica was uncomfortably close to the force field, her face just inches away from the bouncing lightning, and her fingers dangerously close as she worked at the outside slits. She wedged the knife in and gently pushed up. She was conscientious not to exert too much pressure on the blade or the floor panel. She did not want to slip and accidentally touch the force field with her knife tip.

After several long minutes, she finally backed away.

"Well," she said as she stood. "I peeled away enough of the panel," she continued, stretching her limbs. "to know that if I keep trying to get into the guts of the thing, it will take forever, and I'm willing to bet that someone will walk in before I can make any progress. But I have an idea. No guarantee it will work because I am not very familiar with this technology, but it might work. I don't know. I don't think you are going to like it either,"

"What is it?" Aurik asked.

"Well, if I can connect the panel with the force field, there is a possibility that it could short out the force field."

"Wait a minute," Kyle replied. "This whole place is metal. Won't it shock us, too? You know, metal?" He circled his hands around the floor.

"I said you weren't going to like it. There is a very small chance that it won't do anything to us at all."

"Do it. We need to get out of here," Aurik ordered. Jessica nodded and knelt down by the force field.

"Ah, man," Kyle protested.

Jessica balanced the edge of the knife on the panel, readied herself, then let go of it. The knife fell over, the opposite side of the blade contacting the force field with a crackle and a pop, as Jessica hurried away.

The knife shot past her and clanged into the far wall. The force field flickered, and the lightning vanished.

"Come on!" Jessica ordered as she darted across the threshold, Yin, and Sarah right behind her.

Kyle stood in shock, fully expecting to be electrocuted and thrown against the wall as he had been before.

"What happened?" He asked.

Jessica found the control panel for the cells and, after a moment of investigating, turned off the door to Aurik and Kyle's cell.

"Looks like that slim chance of that force field doing nothing to us happened," Jessica replied.

Aurik opened the door to the corridor and peered down both ways.

"Come on. There's a room just down here," he ordered as he darted down the corridor.

Aurik stopped at the door entrance, and it hissed open. The five rushed in.

The N'Roth were busily working, and most of them paid no attention as the five rushed in. Two aliens working at consoles near the door did spot the five, and a third making its way across the room noticed them as well. They were the first three to be knocked out. The last five N'Roth heard the commotion and screams of their counterparts and panicked as they realized what was happening.

The five humans downed the closest two of the remaining aliens almost the instant they looked up from their work. The last three tried futilely to fight their attackers but found themselves unconscious on the floor seconds later.

"Jessica, take care of that door," Aurik ordered. Without hesitation, Jessica headed for the door and began manipulating the controls.

"Everybody, take a station and see if you can make heads or tails out of them," Aurik ordered. They all began searching through the ship's databases, each at a different terminal.

Although they had learned the basics of the N'Roth language in training for their mission, translating the information on the consoles proved difficult.

After a few minutes, Jessica, who had successfully figured out how to lock the door, pulled up a schematic from the main terminal along the wall.

"Over here!" She exclaimed. "Look." The rest of the squad circled around her.

"Are we on a ship?" Yin asked.

"Looks like it," Jessica replied. "I think we are here." She pointed to a small room on the schematic. She moved her finger over the schematic a few inches. "That looks like the brig,"

"Okay, we're on a ship. Where is the hanger bay, then?" Aurik asked.

Jessica zoomed the schematic out, and after a moment, pointed to the rear section. "I think that's it," she said.

"That's a long way. How are we going to get all the way over there?" Kyle asked.

"We might be able to make it most of the way using the maintenance tunnels," Jessica explained as she pointed to a section of lines, following the lines with her finger. "It looks like there is one that runs pretty close to the hangar bay. It looks like we can get in from here." She pointed back toward their location. "I don't think it's far from here,"

"Okay. Put up the maintenance tunnel we need to use," Aurik ordered. Jessica nodded, and a few seconds later, the specific maintenance tunnel route appeared.

"We can access it from here." She pointed again. "Right around the corner,"

"Okay. Let's try and not to be seen. The longer they don't know we have escaped, the better," Aurik said.

The squad of five raced down the corridor toward the maintenance hatch and rounded the corner right into a pair of N'Roth. Seconds later, they were continuing down the corridor, Kyle, and Aurik dragging the aliens with them. Jessica unlatched the maintenance tunnel, and the five climbed in, Aurik and Kyle dragging the unconscious N'Roth with them still.

Once inside, Aurik shut and re-latched the door, then ripped the sleeves off of one of the N'Roth's uniforms and tied their hands and feet together. When he was sufficiently satisfied that they were secure, Aurik stood.

The maintenance tunnel itself was less of a tunnel and more of a corridor. Though they could not stand straight up without hitting their heads on the ceiling beams, they didn't have to crawl. They leaned forward as they walked.

The N'Roth ship was not very intricately designed. It was shaped more or less like a rectangle. This made it easier to get around, that was certain, as the squad learned quickly. The schematics showed only two left turns to get to the hangar bay, one of those turns was after the maintenance tunnel.

Although they were still in only their undergarments, they were not cold. It seemed that these maintenance tunnels were even warmer than the rest of the ship. The N'Roth preferred warmer climates, that much the squad already knew, but the tunnels seemed to be stifling hot, and they were now sweating. Of course, this was partly because of the intensity of the situation in which they found themselves. They still needed to complete their mission or the entire human race would be in jeopardy. They needed to find their ship and escape.

They finally reached the hatch, which was their exit when they heard an alarm.

"Well, they know we escaped, I guess," Kyle remarked.

"Everybody Ready?" Jessica asked, ignoring Kyle, as she readied to unlatch the hatch.

They all nodded.

Jessica cracked the hatch and peered down the corridor. "It's clear," she said and jumped out of the maintenance hatch, followed by the rest of the squad.

Just before they rounded the corner into the corridor that the door to the hangar bay was located, several N'Roth soldiers appeared behind them and, upon seeing the humans, opened fire.

Kyle let out a scream of pain as a rifle blast struck him in the back of his lower shoulder. He tumbled to the floor in a heap.

3

Kyle's body flooded with pain as he hit the floor, hard. His shoulder felt as if a thousand knives had stabbed him. Sharp and intense, unlike anything he had ever felt before. He smelled the stench of burning flesh and then felt the burning of his shoulder. His thoughts were engulfed in his pain, and he couldn't think of anything else. Then he felt a hand grab him.

Aurik picked Kyle up, helping him back to his feet. The two raced down the corridor as the rest of the squad reached the hangar bay door. Luckily, the N'Roth had not yet locked down the ship, and the door hissed open. They all rushed in, Kyle and Aurik just in time to narrowly dodge an onslaught of rifle blasts. Kyle could barely think of anything but the unbelievably excruciating pain.

Kyle more stumbled than ran into the hangar bay, as his shoulder surged with pain with every movement. He grimaced with every fresh pang and winced at every minute movement. His mind flooded with agony, and he could barely concentrate. He wanted to scream out but refused to allow the N'Roth the satisfaction of knowing how much suffering he was in.

He leaned against a bulkhead as much for rest as to steady himself. He leaned into it with a grimace, closing his eyes, wishing for relief from his throbbing shoulder. He had never felt such agony before. Not like this. He fought back the pain and lifted himself off of the bulkhead.

Aurik, Jessica, and Sarah each raced for the first N'Roth they saw, while Yin stayed back, flattening herself against the opposite bulkhead from Kyle, next to the door. Seconds later, a half dozen armed N'Roth charged in, their weapons raised. Yin disarmed the first, catching it off guard, with an elbow to the face, then rushed the second. It, too, was caught off guard as Yin kicked it in the face with a spin kick. The two N'Roth stumbled backward as the remaining four turned their attention to her. She was close enough to the first to grab its rifle and sweep its leg out from under it, dropping the alien to the floor. She kept a tight hold of the soldier's weapon, falling forward with it. Then, at the last second, Yin kicked her feet up into an overhead cartwheel, landing upright next to her fourth victim. She did this so fast that by the time the N'Roth realized what had happened to its counterpart, Yin had already grabbed the alien's rifle bearing arm, spun around towards an adjacent N'Roth, pulling it with her, and flung the alien into its comrade. She finished with a jump kick to its back and a wide swing with her newly acquired rifle into the face of the fourth N'Roth. Both aliens fell to the floor in a heap.

The fifth N'Roth, now within arm's reach, swung the butt of its rifle toward her face. Yin blocked it with her forearms, sidestepping toward the alien and smashing an elbow to the side of its face. The N'Roth stumbled sideways as she twisted her foe's hand, slamming her fist down into its elbow. She heard the sickening crack of bone, and her enemy let out a howl of pain.

She turned for the sixth N'Roth soldier only to find it on the ground with Kyle crouching over it, beating the alien with its own weapon.

Kyle finally stopped and looked up.

"I got him for you," he said with a smile and then nodded behind her.

She immediately spun around and finished the two N'Roth unwise enough to attempt to re-engage her in combat. The N'Roth whose arm she'd broken scrambled away down the corridor.

When she turned back to Kyle, he lay against the bulkhead, sweating and looking pale.

"Kyle, are you okay?" she asked as she knelt beside him.

"Well, I got shot, but other than that, I'm peachy," he replied.

"Come on, let's go," she said, lifting him up.

She glanced around, noticing Aurik, Jessica, and Sarah all in combat of their own. The hangar bay was massive. It looked to be at least three levels high and about several hundred yards wide. There were half a dozen small ships and smaller shuttles. She picked the closest, a shuttle, and headed straight for it.

The shuttle ramp was down, as were most of the shuttles' ramps, and she hauled Kyle up the ramp, plopping him in the first seat she saw.

"Stay here," she ordered. I'm going to help the others. Kyle was in no state to argue, so he just leaned back, keeping off of his wounded shoulder. Yin darted out of the shuttle only to run right back in.

"Okay, we're in trouble," she said.

"Think, what to do," she said, more to herself than Kyle, as she glanced around.

"Kyle, do you think you are well enough to fly this thing?"

"Probably not," he replied as he stood, closing his eyes in pain. She understood.

"Okay, let's hope this thing doesn't have some sort of security access or anything," she replied

Kyle made his way to the pilot's chair and stared at the controls. Protruding from the console were two piloting throttles, each with a large oval-shaped top.

"What's the deal with the N'Roth and ovals?" Kyle asked as he gripped the tops.

"Easier for them to use, maybe."

"Pretty sure these are the piloting throttles," Kyle added, ignoring her reply.

"Let's see if there are any weapons in here," Yin commented and started pulling and yanking on anything that might have looked like a door or storage. She finally found a panel that opened to reveal a locker containing four of the oval-shaped pistol-like weapons she had seen when they were in the prison cells.

"Yes!" she exclaimed and snatched one up, taking a moment to investigate it. She put her fingers in the three notches meant for the N'Roth pinchers. She had to use both hands to hold the weapon, placing her right hand on top with her thumb in the notch that contained what she assumed to be the trigger. With her left hand, she held the oval pistol steady, gripping it by its bottom.

"Okay, Kyle, try and see if you can start this after I leave." Kyle nodded.

Yin peeked out of the rear of the shuttle, noticing Aurik, Sarah, and Jessica, all on their knees with a dozen armed N'Roth surrounding them. She glanced around the hangar bay and found no more N'Roth, so she quickly dropped over the edge of the ramp and darted behind the shuttle, where the N'Roth could not see her. She swiftly made her way to the front of the shuttle and waved to Kyle to start it up, then disappeared out of his view.

Kyle fumbled with a few displays until he heard the hum of the ship powering up. After a few more moments, he found the engine display and powered it on. The hum grew into a faint mechanical roar as the engines powered on. Kyle immediately began manipulating the two piloting throttles, and the shuttle lurched into motion.

Yin crept her way to the nearest obstacle she dared to; she did not want to get spotted, so she knelt behind what looked like a power generator. As she did this, the shuttle Kyle was piloting lurched forward then upward, and back down, slamming into the floor, then scraping against the cold metal surface as it turned. She ignored the ear-piercing screech of metal on metal as best she could, cringing, despite her efforts.

She peeked out from behind her cover and noticed only three N'Roth guarding her friends. As stealthily as she could, she aimed the alien pistol at the middle guard and fired. She was surprised at the lack of recoil this weapon had, even for an energy weapon. A blue energy blast shot from its oval-shaped barrel, hitting its unsuspecting target square in the chest. The N'Roth soldier fell to his back, his chest smoking, and his clothes around the wound melted to his flesh. The wound began to seep blood.

The two N'Roth on either side hesitated in surprise as they saw their counterpart fall on its back. By the time they realized what had happened, it was too late. They turned back to Aurik, Jessica, and Sarah, who were already on top of them.

The two N'Roth weren't even able to bring their weapons up for defense before the three humans disarmed and knocked them out.

Yin raced to their sides.

"Glad to see you," Jessica commented as she snatched up the fallen soldier's weapon.

They heard a loud crash, and the shuttle closest to them slid with an ear-piercing scrape. Suddenly, another one slammed into the bulkhead near the entrance that they had entered through, then reversed and slammed into yet a third shuttle.

"Come on," Yin ordered. She led the four out into the open, peeking around the closest shuttle first, and darting toward the small spacecraft that was colliding with every ship or wall around it.

The four noticed several N'Roth bodies sprawled on the floor. Some were bleeding profusely; others didn't seem injured, though the four knew they were. They all understood now why Kyle had been crashing into everything.

Three N'Roth darted out from the cover of another shuttle, opening fire upon seeing the humans, but not before Yin fired. The first alien went down quickly as the remaining two aliens fired shot after shot, causing the four to scatter behind cover.

Just then, a shuttle slammed into the two N'Roth, and they fell in a heap, their rifles sliding across the hangar floor.

Kyle maneuvered the shuttle so that the rear faced the four and let the ramp down. The four raced for the ship, closing the shuttle's ramp just as another dozen N'Roth soldiers entered the hangar bay.

The five heard the energy blasts start hitting the shuttle just as the ramp closed. Yin was about to yell at Kyle to get them off the ship, but she saw that he had slumped over in the pilot's chair.

"Kyle!" she hollered, her concern allowing more of her accent to filter through her voice.

The squad immediately rushed over to help him, Jessica taking the pilot's chair.

"You guys might want to strap in," she suggested. The squad was already ahead of her, securing Kyle into the seat, then strapping themselves in.

The barrage of weapons fire echoed through the shuttle as they began to move. Jessica raised the shuttle almost to the ceiling, then piloted it down the length of the hangar bay.

"Guys. Hold on. This might not be such a good idea," she explained as she reversed the shuttle until it hit the third level walkway. Then, she punched it as hard as she could.

The shuttle lurched forward, smashing hard into the ship's hangar bay doors with a crash. The pilot's console lit up with warning lights as it slammed into the door.

The door itself bent outward from the force of the shuttle, revealing the dead of space. Lights and warnings erupted throughout the hangar bay as the small crack in the door resulted in any loose object, including the N'Roth being sucked out toward it. A second later, a force field that spanned the length of the hangar bay just behind the door shimmered into existence. Everything fell back down to the floor, including the N'Roth, now unconscious or dead from the fall.

Jessica backed up the shuttle, backing out of the force field. The force field had deployed to re-pressurize the hangar bay and was not designed to stop physical objects from passing through it. She punched it forward again, full throttle, slamming into the outer hull cargo bay door again. This time, the shuttle did not stop. It broke through the door with another loud crash, slowing slightly, then gaining momentum again when it cleared the door. Every single light illuminated on the pilot's console this time, and warning beeps sounded as if the small spacecraft were playing a symphony.

Jessica kept the engines at full power, trying to get as far away from the N'Roth ship as she could. Then she fiddled with the controls until a display of planets popped up on the shuttle's windshield. The display was barely readable, blinking, and phasing in and out with static so she could not read the N'Roth words on the display. She picked a planet at random, the display vanished, and they jumped into lightspeed.

"Okay, we should be good for a while. I'm pretty sure we can't be tracked in lightspeed," Jessica explained. "How is Kyle?" she asked.

"Not good," Yin replied. "He doesn't seem to be able to focus, and he can't think clearly. He's getting sick or something."

"It has to do with that energy blast that hit him in the shoulder," Aurik said.

"We need to take a look at it and dress it," Sarah said. "I'm sure the N'Roth keep an emergency medical kit or something in here, just in case."

"Over here," Yin said as she jumped up, rushing over to the panel under which she had found the N'Roth pistols. "There might be something in one of these panels," she explained as she began popping off the panels below the uncovered weapons container.

The first panel held food rations, and the second held what they were hoping for. Yin started pulling everything out of the container, handing it to Sarah and Aurik, who inspected each of the supply cases.

"I can't make heads or tails out of most of this stuff," Aurik complained.

"These, you could say, are bandages. One side feels a little sticky, and it looks like the clothing they wear," Sarah explained.

"What about antiseptic?" Jessica asked.

"Well, there are a lot of bottles in here," Aurik began. "But I can't make out half of these N'Roth words on them." He snatched up a couple of the bottles with clear liquid in them, opened the lids, and sniffed the contents. He jerked his head back after inhaling the second. "This has got to be antiseptic of some kind." He passed it to Sarah, who gently sniffed it.

"Whoa. I think your right," she said. "It smells like a combination of whiskey and rubbing alcohol."

"Well, I hope so," Jessica replied. "Let's see what happens if we pour it on his wound."

Yin returned to Kyle's side and was about to speak when he lifted his head up. "Can someone please stop that infernal noise? It's killing me!" Nobody missed the irony. Even in pain and sickness, he kept his sense of humor.

"I'll try," Jessica replied and went back to manipulating the console.

"Kyle, we are going to try and dress your wound, so it doesn't get worse, okay," Yin explained. Kyle nodded.

"I'm not sure it can get any worse," he replied.

Aurik slowly poured the antiseptic on Kyle's wound. The moment it touched Kyle's shoulder, he let out a scream of complete agony, then passed out, his body going limp. Aurik stopped pouring the moment Kyle screamed, and Yin checked for Kyle's pulse when he fell limp. She nodded to the others in relief when she found it.

"He must have passed out from the pain," Sarah commented, then noticed Kyle's shoulder. "Look." She pointed to Kyle's wound.

The liquid had started bubbling and foaming as it ran down Kyles wound.

"Well, I think that is a good sign. It looks like it is cleaning his wound," Aurik said. Without warning, he dumped the rest of the liquid on Kyle's shoulder. It bubbled and foamed, and when it had finished, the wound did indeed look clean. They bandaged the wound with what they could find in the first aid kit, and Jessica figured out how to turn off all of the warning signals.

She waited until they had finished bandaging Kyle's shoulder before she spoke.

"I've got some very bad news," she said gravely. "All those alarms that were going off, well, they were basically telling us that the hull integrity is failing. The engines are about to give out on us, and we are draining power quickly. We'll be dead in the water in under fifteen minutes."

The crew looked at each other solemnly.

"Maybe if we drop out of lightspeed, we can buy ourselves more time, but I don't know how much," she added.

"Drop out of lightspeed. With any luck, we will drop out close enough to one of those planets you had on the display," Aurik ordered.

"Yes sir," Jessica replied and dropped them out of lightspeed. "Aurik," she added. "I noticed, when that display of planets came on, there was a list of hundreds of habitable planets, not just those four shown. They were just the closest."

They dropped out of lightspeed.

"How can that be? We only had a couple of colonized planets when we left," Aurik replied as he came up beside her. He leaned over her chair, one hand on the console and the other on the back of her chair, and peered out the windshield.

"I know. Something weird is definitely going on here," she replied as she manipulated the console again. A planet popped up on the display, still blinking and phasing in and out with static.

"Setting a course for that planet," she reported. Aurik could see the distant stars move sideways as the shuttle altered course.

Jessica worked the console again, and moments later sighed. "Doesn't look like we saved too much of our power. If I'm reading this right, we only added about ten more minutes. The course change may have had something to do with it," she informed.

***

Fifteen minutes later, the shuttle entered the planet's atmosphere, and immediately the cabin power shut off.

"I thought we had more time," Aurik commented.

Jessica rapped on the console panel.

"The shuttle diverted power to the hull plating to keep it from getting more damage on our entry, and we are using a lot of power to slow our descent," she explained

Just then, the console went dark.

"We are draining too much power. Everything is shutting down. Brace yourselves; if we make it to the ground, it won't be a nice landing," she reported.

The four braced themselves, Yin trying to keep Kyle from injuring himself as he sat unconscious in his seat.

They stared out the shuttle windshield, helpless, watching the orange flames of the atmosphere collide with the hull of the shuttle.

Then, as quickly as the flames started, they stopped.

Then the hull cracked wide open.

They could feel the cold air rushing in.

The atmosphere was thin, and they had difficulty breathing.

The crack grew wider.

The wind smacked hard against their bare skin and faces.

The ground grew larger and larger before them.

They saw the tops of the trees growing larger.

They watched as their deaths approached.

The treetops came fast.

They felt the pounding of the tips of the treetops as they plummeted into the forest below.

They saw the trees engulf them.

They felt the jerking of the shuttle bouncing against the trees.

The last thing they saw and felt before everything went black was the massive structure in the middle of the forest and a jarring so intense that brought with it a wave of pain.

4

Kyle awoke to fresh pain, and as he looked down, he noticed a branch protruding from his calf. He moved to get a better look at this new wound, and an eruption of pain surged through his shoulder, reminding him of the blast wound he'd received.

"Why does this keep happening to me?" he asked.

He fought through the pain, every minuscule movement sending fresh surges of pain through his shoulder and his leg. He unlatched the seatbelt holding him in his chair and stood up, keeping his weight on his good leg. Fresh waves of almost debilitating pain flooded through him, and he found it hard to concentrate. He took hold of the chair near him to steady himself.

The shuttle had broken apart. One entire side of the shuttle had been ripped off, revealing the forest beyond.

Jessica and Aurik sat unconscious at the two pilots'
chairs, part of the console ripped up and shoved toward them
by a massive tree branch that had broken through the shuttle
windshield, which had sprayed glass shards throughout the
shuttle.

Yin sat beside him, bleeding from cuts from the glass
shards, as did Sarah, who sat unconscious opposite Yin.

He leaned toward Yin to try to shake her awake, but
instead, the shuttle began to spin as a new wave of pain
engulfed him, and he fell into her lap, his head throbbing. Yin
woke as a result of Kyle falling on her, and she immediately
lifted him back to his seat, ignoring the aching from the million
cuts she had throughout her body.

"Kyle, are you okay?" she asked.

"You mean besides being shot in the shoulder, a
splitting headache, and a branch through my leg?" he replied.

"What?" she exclaimed and sat forward to look at his
leg. The seatbelt prevented her from doing so. She quickly

unlatched it and stood, ignoring the pain from the cuts along her body.

She stared at it when she saw it, unsure of what to do, then she heard the moaning of Aurik as he stirred.

"Don't move, Kyle," she said and started to move around Kyle, then froze, hissing.

"Don't got to worry about me moving an inch," he replied.

She looked down to see the shuttle floor littered with glass shards from the windshield. She moved her bare foot off of a couple of shards and gently brushed them aside.

"Aurik, anything broken?" she asked as she carefully made her way to his side, brushing away the glass shards in her path.

He woke fully, immediately feeling his fresh cuts and sore face.

"Nothing broken, but every inch of me hurts," he replied.

"Be careful where you step," she said and made her way to Jessica, gently shaking her awake. Upon waking Jessica, she informed her and Sarah, who had started to stir by now, as well, of the glass shards.

The squad spent a few minutes gathering their senses, and then Aurik took a sitrep, learning of Kyle's newest injury, which he knew would become deadly if they didn't figure out a way to heal it soon. He didn't want to remove the branch that somehow made its way, literally, through Kyle's calf.

They cleared a path through the shards of glass and gathered outside, Yin and Aurik helping Kyle.

"I saw a settlement as we were crashing," Jessica said. "I'm not sure how far away it is, but it's that way." She pointed.

Aurik nodded.

"We'll help Kyle; you lead the way," he said.

The hike was laborious and torturous as they were all still barefoot. The N'Roth never bothered to give them any clothes, and they still only wore undergarments.

It was hot, and they had no water. They had escaped the N'Roth ship successfully and survived their shuttle crash; now, they had to survive the wilderness with literally nothing. They hadn't taken any of the alien rations because they weren't sure what it was or how their bodies would react to the foreign food.

With every few steps, they were stepping on a thorn, sharp twig, or pebble. It was even worse for Aurik and Yin, who carried Kyle along as he hobbled on his one good leg, depending on the two of them for support.

Within a half-hour, they had to stop and rest, their feet cut, sore, and bruised. They rested for a few minutes keeping off of their bare, bruised, and torn feet, relishing in the few moments of relief. They were all soaked in sweat, and their dirty, black undergarments stuck to their bodies like saran wrap. They were beginning to get dehydrated as they hadn't had food or water since they woke up from stasis.

They stood finally, Aurik and Yin helping Kyle to his feet and securing him between them so they could help him walk.

Minutes later, they luckily found a heavily used trail and followed it. Shortly after finding the path, they came to a clearing that opened up into farmland. Sarah and Jessica knelt low, and Aurik and Yin concealed themselves in the trees. They were up on a hill overlooking a valley. They could see off in the distance a house near the edge of a cornfield. After they observed their surroundings sufficiently, they returned to the others in the trees. They discussed their plan, relaying the layout of the valley to Aurik, Yin, and Kyle. After a few minutes, they decided they would follow the tree line as close as they could to the cornfield, where the hill was lowest, and make their way toward the house. They had not initially seen anyone working in the fields. However, they had noticed smoke rising from the chimney of the house, so they decided they would seek help from the occupants of the farm.

They reached the farmhouse, and Sarah knocked on the door. Jessica was behind her with Aurik, Yin, and Kyle behind Jessica. They heard heavy footsteps inside the house, and the door creaked open. A grey-bearded man in his sixties opened the door with a look of surprise as he saw the five in their undergarments.

"Sir," Sarah began, "our friend is very injured and needs medical attention. May we impose on you to take us to the nearest medical facility?"

The old man looked them each up and down as Sarah spoke, and before she had finished, opened the door wide for them to enter.

"Set him on the bed in the back room," he said.

"Thank you, sir," Sarah replied and led the four into the back room.

The old man shut the door, grabbed a medical kit from another room, and followed the five into the bedroom.

The squad saw him enter with the medical kit and gave him room, recognizing many of the items as he opened the kit, and glanced at each other curiously. They watched as the old man observed Kyle's leg and shoulder. He chose to address the leg first.

He took out two vials containing clear liquid, set one aside, and handed the other to Sarah.

"Have him drink this," he said.

Sarah moved around the bed to Kyles' head and gently aided him in drinking the liquid.

The old man pulled out a quarter-sized sphere from the kit, then a metallic needle-like poker. He impaled the white sphere with the poker until it sat securely on its tip.

"Hold this." He gave the needle-like poker to Jessica, who stood next to him. "Come around here." He motioned for her to move to his other side. "When I take this branch out, shove the ball into his wound quickly," he said.

Jessica nodded. He yanked the branch out, releasing a slight moan from Kyle, who looked as if he hadn't a care in the world. Blood began to squirt and flow. Jessica shoved the sphere into Kyle's gushing wound, and almost instantaneously, the white ball turned red and expanded, filling up the gaping wound.

The old man wrapped Kyle's leg with a bandage. It was identical to the dressing they had used to cover Kyle's shoulder. Again, the squad gave each other curious glances.

When he finished bandaging Kyle's leg, he moved to Kyle's shoulder.

"How did you clean this?" he asked.

"We poured one of those clear vials on it," Aurik replied. The man looked up.

"You poured it on him?" Aurik nodded.

"That explains it," he said.

"Explains what?" Aurik asked.

"Look," the man said, backing away. Aurik moved closer to Kyle to take a look at his shoulder. It had blistered.

"You used too much. It should have healed, but because you used too much, the excess liquid got trapped underneath his new skin. We'll have to pop the blisters and let them heal naturally. He will have scars there, as well as on his leg, most likely. Unless you want to take him to the N'Roth medical facility, but the blast wound to your friend's shoulder here, and, well, your appearance tells me you probably would rather not," he said as he moved close to Kyle's shoulder and began attending to it.

"I didn't think so," he said after a moment of silence. "There are some clothes in the next room and a washbasin. Clean yourselves off and get some clothes, and I'll attend to your injuries and your feet when I'm done here. You're getting blood all over my floor," he added.

The four looked down at their feet and the floor. They had almost forgotten about their cuts and bruises; they had become so used to the pain. They looked around, noticing a path of blood smears where they had been walking.

"Sorry about that," Aurik said. "Thank you for everything you are doing."

The old man nodded.

The four washed and helped themselves to the man's clothes. After Aurik had finished washing, he returned to Kyle's room, pulling on a shirt, having already donned trousers.

"He will be fine in a few days. He's all drugged up and sleeping right now, but he'll be fine," the old man said as Aurik walked in. Aurik nodded.

"Sir, may I ask what you are doing with N'Roth medical supplies?" Aurik asked.

"What do you mean? It's standard medical equipment," he replied. "Like everything else N'Roth. Where are you from?" The man asked, furrowing his brow.

"Earth."

"Ha, that's impossible. What are you doing way out here?"

"What do you mean?"

"How did you get here, I mean. You are obviously on the run, but there's no way you could have gotten all the way here on the run from Earth. Not through the heart of N'Roth

occupied territory."

At this, Aurik's own confusion showed.

"Who are you?" The old man asked.

"What do you mean, occupied territory?" Aurik asked.

"You really don't know?"

Aurik shook his head.

"Where have you been for the past two hundred years?"

Aurik's face lit up with exasperation at the comment,

realization finally setting in.

"Two hundred years, what do you mean? What

happened two hundred years ago?"

"Well, we surrendered. We were concurred."

Aurik stared at him.

"Son, who are you?"

Aurik soaked in the revelation, putting two and two

together. It all made sense: waking up on the ship, the list of

inhabited planets, the N'Roth interrogating them.

When he finally spoke, Aurik explained their mission from Earth during the war, being put into stasis, and waking up on the N'Roth ship. They had been in stasis for over two hundred years rather than a mere few months. They had failed their mission.

After that, the old man gave the squad a brief history lesson, explaining that the humans had lost the war with the N'Roth. The N'Roth colonized Earth and spread what was left of the human race over about a hundred or so planets. The N'Roth had occupied Earth's solar system and surrounding solar systems, making Earth an N'Roth military planet. The humans were put into labor camps on various worlds and forced to serve the N'Roth farming and working. He explained that they were on the outskirts of the N'Roth territory, so there was not very much N'Roth presence on the planet, except for the station a few miles away conducting routine patrols and inspections to "keep the peace."

The squad took it all in as he spoke, their minds racing in every direction as they contemplated the ramifications of all that they heard.

***

The next day, the old man, Benjamin, woke as he usually did for the beginning of the farming week and prepared breakfast.

Kyle's shoulder was feeling almost as good as new, and his calf was throbbing but no longer felt as though he had been impaled.

The rest of the squad had not yet woken but soon woke to the smells of bacon and eggs. They had come to terms with the revelation that the human race had been enslaved, and after a lengthy discussion, they decided they would not just lie down and assimilate into this new existence of servitude and a conquered people.

Benjamin had explained that all humans were given an identity chip placed in their forearm at the age of five, and if they were caught without it, they could be imprisoned or put to death, so they couldn't go into the city.

He had offered to show them a well-hidden cave he knew of that was just a couple of miles into the forest, but they would have to wait until dark when the workers had left.

"Ah, good morning. Breakfast is almost done," Benjamin said as he noticed them stirring in their makeshift beds strewn about the living area.

"Smells delicious," Sarah replied, the rest agreeing.

Benjamin finished cooking breakfast and motioned toward several plates and cups set on the table. The squad served themselves breakfast at Benjamin's prodding as he delivered a plate to Kyle, who still lay in bed, the effects of the drugs still not entirely worn off.

"I'll be going to town today to get you supplies," he said as he returned. "When it gets dark, I'll take you to that cave I told you about yesterday. No doubt, the N'Roth would have at least sent word to keep an eye out for you." The squad nodded as they stuffed their faces with breakfast.

Soon, Benjamin was about his daily business, supervising the work in the fields among his other daily duties.

The squad spent the day cooped up in Benjamin's crowded home. When Kyle appeared lucid enough, they relayed to him everything Benjamin had explained. Kyle took the news about as well as the rest of them had, then agreed with his comrades that they weren't just going to lie down.

They began planning what to do next. First, they needed weapons and shelter, which, hopefully, Benjamin's cave would supply the shelter. The weapons they left in the shuttle they crash-landed in would begin their supply, and the five would strip the shuttle of what they could that might help them. Jessica had explained that generally sensors—unless the N'Roth had significantly improved them in the two hundred years they were in stasis—were not very strong and could not penetrate solid rock, so at the very least, the N'Roth wouldn't be able to find them in the cave.

***

Night finally fell, and Benjamin led them through the forest to the cave. The hike was slow due to the lack of light, as well as Kyle's injury. Though his leg was healing, it was still very sore and painful to walk on, but he refused to be cooped up in the house any longer.

"Let's see," Benjamin said. "Where's that entrance?" He glanced around, trying to remember. "I haven't been out here since I was a kid. It's around here somewhere."

He spent several moments searching through the overgrown shrubbery, looking for the familiar cleft between one of the trees and a large boulder that protruded out from the cliffside.

"Ah! Here it is," Benjamin exclaimed as he lifted a thick, densely grown branch aside. They all took notice that the rock looked as if the cliff had grown around it as it protruded, literally, from inside the cliff face. "Looks like the forest has grown. I don't remember this tree being so full, or this place being so hard to find," he said as he squeezed himself into the small space.

The rock, tree, and cliff were indeed deceptive. From the looks of it, the opening appeared only as a cleft. When they climbed into the cleft, however, it dropped into a massive cavern a good twenty to thirty square feet large.

"There are more rooms down that way," Benjamin reported as he shone his flashlight across the cavern. "There are even more rooms deeper in the cave, but I was never brave enough to go that far."

The five slowly shone their flashlights across the cavern, examining the space. Small sections of the cavern opened up into more rooms of varying sizes, and there were a few tunnels that led farther than their flashlights could shine.

"Alright, let's check this place out. Kyle, Sarah, Yin, take that side." Aurik flashed his light to the opposite side of the cavern. "Benjamin, Jessica, and I will take this side." The three nodded and began investigating the rooms and tunnels while Benjamin led Aurik and Jessica into the next chamber.

"I used to come in here to get away from it all. The N'Roth, the work, my parents," he said as he led them into the next chamber. He shone his flashlight in the corner of the chamber, finding an old, rotted sleeping bag. "I used to sleep there on occasion when I was really upset," he shone the flashlight directly ahead of them. "That's the next room," he said.

The chamber wall opened into an opening several feet wide into another room, spanning about seventy to eighty square feet. The far wall beyond that opened up into smaller compartments, and several tunnels extended beyond the rooms at varying lengths. Some connected rooms together, and others opened up into new chambers. They didn't venture far for fear they would get lost in the labyrinth of tunnels.

When Aurik, Jessica, and Benjamin returned to the central chamber, they found the others waiting on them.

"How does your side look?" asked Aurik.

"There are so many tunnels, ya'll wouldn't believe," Kyle replied.

"Oh, we'd believe," Aurik said. "There's a labyrinth on our side, too. We'll have to create a map or something, so we don't get lost."

"Yup. It's big. We could make it cozy," Kyle said.

"It's agreed, then?" Aurik asked.

"Yup," Kyle said.

"Good enough for me," replied Sarah.

"Yep," Jessica answered.

"It's a little dirty, but I guess it will do," Yin said with a smirk.

"Alright," Aurik said. "We stay here tonight."

"You guys are really going to do this?" Benjamin asked.

They all nodded.

"Okay, well, if you need anything, I'll help when I can. I hope you all know what you are doing."

"So do we," Kyle said.

"Thanks for all that you have done for us, Benjamin. We will repay you someday," Aurik said.

Benjamin extended a hand.

"I'm going to start heading back. I hope the best for you and your cause." They each shook Benjamin's hand and thanked him, then Benjamin climbed out of the cave, disappearing into the night.

"Alright, let's start setting up what we have. Tomorrow, we will get what we can from the shuttle," Aurik said. The squad nodded and went to unpacking the supplies Benjamin had procured from town.

They each had sleeping gear and food, as well as a couple of changes of clothes. Benjamin had provided a handful of pots and pans and a medical kit for them, explaining its contents. He had given them boots in their sizes that he had bought in town, along with the clothes.

After they had decided where they were going to sleep for the night, they each found their sleep rather quickly.

5

They woke late the next morning, partially because very little light seeped in from the opening of the musty cave, so the morning light hadn't wakened them as it did the day before in Benjamin's home.

When the first couple of squad members did finally wake, they prepared breakfast near the entrance of the cave, rousing the rest of the squad with the aroma of a well-cooked breakfast.

They sat virtually in silence, except for a few comments here and there, or a compliment on the cooking.

They had set up their flashlights around their makeshift kitchen, so they could see better while cooking and eating. The meal didn't take long, and they were soon on their hike to the crashed shuttle to salvage what they could.

They emptied the packs Benjamin had provided them, only taking water so they could pack as much into their packs as possible and take fewer treks to the craft.

They left Kyle in the cave, mainly because of his leg, suggesting that he explore the cave if he wanted something to do.

***

It was a two-mile hike, and they were all well-fed and healthy, so it didn't take them long to reach the crashed shuttle, unlike when they crash-landed. When they finally reached the shuttle, they immediately started salvaging for supplies, starting with the weapons, medical kit, and any other smaller items they could find. After that, they moved on to some of the larger items, filling their packs to the brim.

While the rest of the squad was scavenging, Jessica began dismantling the consoles, searching for anything useful. After she dismantled the consoles, she found the shuttle power source, hoping to find a way to recharge it and supply their new secret base with some measure of power.

Before they left, they camouflaged the shuttle, hoping to keep any N'Roth from finding it. They moved as much fallen brush around it as they could and covered the crash landing trail with branches, as well.

They knew that within a few days, the brush would be dead, so they made as many trips as they could before night fell and brought back with every trip more and more supplies, even dragging full sections of consoles that Jessica thought might be useful.

On their second trip, they dismantled much of the seating and hauled them to their base for Kyle to reassemble.

Jessica had even instructed the squad to gut the shuttle of all wires and circuitry so that she could repurpose them.

Kyle had spent most of the day exploring the cave. He scraped along the cave walls and carved arrows in the softer ground of the cave, indicating which way he was going so all he needed to do was follow the arrows in reverse to get back to the entrance. He kept an old-fashioned spiral of notepaper with him, scratching down a crude map of the halls and rooms he explored.

They all went to bed that night exhausted but not before discussing the next day's plans.

***

The next day, they scouted the nearby town, noticing almost no security. It seemed like any other small country town the five of them would have visited before they had gone into stasis, with the exception that it looked more outdated and rundown, almost as if the city itself was a village from ancient times.

"Okay, so we are looking for power supplies and converters," Jessica explained. "For now, the smaller, the better."

"And if ya'll happen to come by some weapons, don't hesitate to snatch 'em," Kyle added.

"If you find anything that might be useful, then see if you can acquire it, but our first priority is the power supplies and converters," Aurik said.

Everyone nodded in understanding.

"Kyle, Yin, and Jessica, you three will take the North side of the town, and Sarah and I will take the South side. Don't get caught; remember what Benjamin said."

They all nodded again.

Aurik tapped Sarah on the shoulder and began South.

***

Aurik and Sarah knelt low, circling the town until they came to a housing section. They kept to the cover of clusters of trees that grew sporadically around the housing section of the city, then darted to the nearest home. It looked much like Benjamin's but much larger.

They kept close to the wall, hoping to keep from being noticed by any occupants who may be in the large cabin.

"Stay close to the walls," Aurik said. "If you see any N'Roth, stay clear of them. Try not to get noticed."

Sarah nodded in reply.

Aurik stepped out from the cover of the cabin and casually walked down the side of the yard and into the housing section of the small town.

***

Kyle, Jessica, and Yin casually made their way to a large grove sectioned off from the city. Once they neared, they snatched up baskets other workers had set down, trying to blend in. They worked their way through the grove and found their way into the city without a problem.

The town wasn't gated or guarded, so they had no problem getting in. There was an N'Roth patrol here and there, but the N'Roth didn't seem to notice or care that they were wandering the town.

They tried to stay inconspicuous, keeping near small pockets of citizens as they went about their business.

Some held baskets as the three of them did, so they started following them until they reached a secluded area and darted into an alleyway between two buildings.

Aurik and Sarah stayed close to the walls of the houses, trying to act casual. As they neared the center of the village, they noticed the neighborhood housing becoming livelier. Young children played in the dirt street, while an occasional adult worked outside their house.

Soon, they reached what appeared to be the market. Farmer's produce booths lined the edges with simple overhangs and crates of various produce. Beyond the produce were stores and shops with solid structures.

The two strolled along the street, observing the produce as if they were customers and taking note of the layout of the area. After a few minutes, they made their way to the shops, casually perusing the shelves, again observing the layout of the shops themselves, looking for any power sources or converters.

They had scanned three shops for power sources, finding none, when they decided to try outside around the back. They ducked into an alley between two shops and found the power generator.

"I knew we should have tried the back first," Sarah said.

"Okay, well, let's be quick. How are we going to get this out?"

"That's easy," Sarah replied. "Watch." She knelt down beside the waist-high, cylindrical power generator, opened a panel, revealing three smaller cylindrical devices about six inches tall and three inches in diameter. She yanked out the first as hard as she could, ripping it from the wiring. The hum of the generator lessened as the power supply diminished.

"Here." She handed the cylinder to Aurik and yanked out the other two, and the generator fell utterly silent.

"Now, we had better get out of here," Sarah said.

The two hurried back through the alleyway, only for Aurik to smack hard into someone rounding the corner.

The two tumbled to the ground, Aurik almost knocking Sarah over as she barely stopped in time to avoid the collision.

"Hey!" the man hollered as he scrambled back to his feet, noticing the power supplies. "Give those back!"

Sarah grabbed the man and shoved him further into the alley as Aurik scrambled to his feet, as well.

The man stumbled several feet, then caught himself on the wall and spun around.

"Thieves!" he yelled, darting out of the alley after the two.

Aurik and Sarah raced down the street, no longer concerned with being inconspicuous. The screaming of their victim bringing every eye in their direction and a pair of patrolling N'Roth soldiers in pursuit.

***

Kyle, Jessica, and Yin found the generator quickly.

"Well, that was easy," Kyle said as Jessica knelt down, opening the panel.

"Three, good," she said and began unhooking the first of the power supplies.

"Okay, let's go," she said, closing the panel.

"Wait, we're not going to get all three?" Yin asked.

"No, this way, they hopefully won't discover it's missing until we are long gone," Jessica replied. "The generator is still getting power this way and will give us time to get more."

Yin nodded.

"Well, to the next one, then," Kyle said.

Five generators later, there was still no sign that any of the missing power supplies had been discovered. They had stayed along the backside of the buildings, moving from generator to generator. They were easily hidden as there was a tall concrete wall opposite the buildings, and unless someone rounded the corner to the back, they were in no danger of being discovered.

"Alright, I think that's enough for now," Jessica said as she stood up, shutting the panel of the generator.

The three casually made their way down the street, noticing a flurry of commotion ahead. They hid the power supplies in a pack, so it wasn't apparent that they had any contraband; however, they all noticed to their dismay that several N'Roth soldiers were snatching up any possessions citizens had and searching them.

Jessica nodded to a nearby alley, and they darted into it. They made their way back to the dead-end wall, taking cover on the back wall of a shop, out of sight.

"Might as well get a power supply from this one while we are here," Jessica said as she knelt to retrieve a power supply.

"We're stuck. It's only a matter of time till we're discovered," Kyle said. "We've got to find another way outta here." Kyle waved for Yin. "Let's see what's over this wall," he said.

Yin nodded as she saw Kyle entangling his fingers together, making a foothold with his hands.

She used his makeshift foothold as a stepping stool onto his shoulders and grabbed onto the edge of the wall. She pulled herself up just enough for her to see what was on the other side and quickly lowered herself, stepping off Kyle's shoulders.

"It looks like an N'Roth compound," she said. "There are several vehicles and crates. A large building on the far side."

"So that way's outta the question," Kyle replied.

6

Aurik and Sarah raced down the street toward the farmer's market, the two N'Roth soldiers in close pursuit. They couldn't just run back out of the town as the market section was walled in, unlike the housing section. Their only hope of escaping the soldiers chasing them was to make it to the housing area.

That option ended as they saw four more N'Roth running toward them from the far end of the market ahead. They knew they couldn't fight past the four before the two chasing them caught up with them.

They darted into the alley and backtracked the way they had come, along the back of the shops, the two N'Roth right behind them. They ran along the back of the shops, and the outer wall for several buildings then darted back down the alley and back into the main street, taking cover on each side of the alleyway entrance, pressing tight against their respective store walls.

Their N'Roth pursuers didn't know what hit them. As they cleared the alleyway, they both received an elbow to the face, sending them to the ground.

Aurik and Sarah were just about to snatch up the N'Roth's weapons when the four soldiers they had seen earlier rounded the back of the alleyway, fleeing instead into the nearest shop, slamming the door shut just as the soldiers emerged from the alley.

The two leaned against the shop wall, bracing for another attack. Seconds passed, and the N'Roth didn't enter. They visibly relaxed, realizing the N'Roth had not seen them enter the store and observed the room. It was a clothing shop with half a dozen customers staring at them.

The two tensed again, unsure how to handle the situation. Aurik smiled, moving away from the door awkwardly. The shoppers stared a few more moments, then went back to their shopping. Aurik and Sarah waited casually for a few minutes, feigning interest in several items then left.

They saw two of the four N'Roth searching through the belongings of citizens while the other two were scanning the crowd.

Aurik and Sarah found a wall to casually lean on as the two N'Roth scanning the street spotted them. They tried to look as if they were engaging in conversation, Aurik keeping an eye on the two N'Roth who didn't seem to recognize them.

A flatbed cargo transport passed by, then. It was small, manned by a single driver, hovering by with an audible hum. It had several dozen crates on board, and it seemed out of place, the one piece of modern technology they had seen since entering this town, other than the power generators.

The driver stopped just past them, blocking the view of the N'Roth soldiers.

"Come on," Aurik said.

"Hey, want some help?" Aurik asked as he neared the vehicle. The driver looked at him, unsure how to respond.

"We're waiting on a friend, bored out of our minds. We've been waiting a while," Aurik bluffed.

The driver nodded.

"Yeah, sure. I've got a few loads for this shop." He pointed to the shop he had pulled up to. "Grab these two and follow me," the driver said, picking up a crate after slapping a palm on similar containers under it, leaning backward to rebalance himself against the added heaviness of the box.

Aurik and Sarah hefted the heavy crates into the shop, following the driver.

"I haven't seen you two around here before. Did you come in on the transport last week? I didn't know they were bringing humans, too," the driver asked as he maneuvered into the back of the shop, dropping the crate onto a stack of more crates.

"Uh, yeah. Still not used to this place," Aurik replied as he and Sarah set their crates next to his.

"Well, they treat us real nice here. As long as you follow the rules, you will be fine. Some of the N'Roth are actually pretty nice," the driver said, zigzagging back through the shop.

"I see. So, where are you going with all of these crates? What's your job?" Aurik asked.

The driver pointed to another stack of crates, picking up the first.

"I pretty much do this all day, sort and deliver orders and supplies wherever they need to go."

"Ah, sounds like you keep busy," Sarah said as she and Aurik each picked up a crate.

"Yeah, most of the time. There are a few months that business is slow, when people aren't buying much, but I don't have a lot of competition here, so not so bad," the driver replied as he entered the shop.

"I see," Sarah said, "so where's your next stop? Anywhere more exciting than this boring section of town?"

The driver set the crate down, helping Sarah and Aurik with theirs.

"Yeah, actually. I'm delivering an order to the N'Roth next. Now, that place is nice," he said, making his way outside again. He snatched up a tablet. "I need to have them sign for this. I'll be right back," he explained and darted back into the shop, returning just a few moments later.

"So, I'm starting to think we might have gotten stood up here," Aurik said. "Do you mind if we hitch a ride with you? We kinda don't want to have to walk."

"Well, yeah. I guess I can drop you off somewhere," the driver replied as he slid into the driver's seat. "Hop into the bed. Where do you need to go?"

"Uh, that way." Aurik pointed behind them, away from the N'Roth patrol searching citizens. "We'll tell you where to stop."

"Alright. Hold on," the driver said, then circled the vehicle around and sped off the way he had come.

***

"I have an idea," Jessica said. "Look around for anything metal." Kyle and Yin began scanning the alley for anything metal. After a moment, Kyle snatched up a short and fat object with jagged edges and handed it to Jessica.

"Perfect," she said, snatching it in a hurry, and began fiddling with the generator wiring.

A few minutes later, she stood.

"Come on," she ordered. "Quickly!" she snapped and raced down the back alleyway. Kyle and Yin followed without hesitation, hearing the urgency in her voice.

Seconds later, the three heard a loud boom.

"Hurry, this way," Jessica said and darted into the joining alley between two stores as Yin and Kyle spun toward the boom behind them to see the generator had exploded and caught fire, dark smoke billowing up.

They spun back around, following Jessica down the alley and into the main street, understanding in full what her plan was. The three slowed to a casual walk, scanning the street.

A crowd gathered near the store Jessica had sabotaged, and all the N'Roth in the vicinity were racing toward the building.

It wasn't hard after that to get out of the town. The three walked out of the market section of the city and back into the grove, then back into the wilderness.

Kyle, Jessica, and Yin were the first group back to the rendezvous, but they didn't have to wait long before Aurik and Sarah met up with them.

"Sorry we took so long. We, uh, had to go a bit out of our way to get back out of the village," Sarah said and handed Jessica her pack. "Here you go. We, uh, couldn't get any more." Jessica took the pack and peered into it then glanced at Aurik and Sarah.

"You only got three?" she asked. "And did you just rip these straight out of the generator?" she asked, pulling one out.

"Seemed like a quick way to get them," Sarah replied. Jessica sighed, irritated.

"Well, if you would have thought things through more, you might have been able to get more," she said.

"How many did you get?" Aurik asked.

"Ten," Jessica replied.

"Ten! How did you manage ten?" Aurik asked.

"Well, when I noticed there were three power supplies in the generator, I only took one from each. That way the power for the buildings didn't turn off," Jessica answered.

"That definitely would have worked better," Aurik said. "Good job in getting so many." He nodded. "Listen, there's a lot of daylight hours left. Sarah and I found out about some kind of transport that came in last week. We're going to see if Benjamin can give us some intel about it." Aurik pointed at Yin and Kyle.

"You two go back with Jessica and help her with whatever she needs help with." They nodded.

"Okay. We'll be back by nightfall," he finished and motioned for Sarah to follow him.

Jessica tossed Sarah's pack to Kyle and smiled.

"You heard him. I'm the boss." Kyle frowned at her as she turned and headed for their base.

***

Aurik and Sarah reached Benjamin's farm, keeping an eye out for any N'Roth as they searched for Benjamin. They finally found him near a barn at the far end of his field.

Benjamin recognized them before they ever neared and dismissed the farm hand he was talking to, who darted off while Benjamin entered the barn.

The two followed him in.

"You two are quite brave, walking around here like you belong here," Benjamin said, leaning against the side of the barn.

"Well, it's worked for us so far," Aurik said. Benjamin narrowed his eyes at the comment.

"Well, no one really cares out here. They probably wouldn't notice you if you were working as one of my farmhands. Nobody pays much attention here."

"Listen, Benjamin, we heard about a transport that came in last week. Do you know anything about that?" Aurik asked.

"How did you hear about that?" Benjamin asked, surprised. "You went into town after I warned you what would happen if you got caught."

Aurik nodded.

Benjamin motioned to several barrels in the corner and walked over to one, rolling it on its edge a few feet, then sat on top of it. Aurik and Sarah did the same.

"Well, every few months or so, the N'Roth bring supply shipments. Food, equipment, and the like."

"Do they bring weapons or people?" Sarah asked.

"Sure, if they were needed, I suppose, but mostly non-military stuff. Maybe a few military office supplies for the N'Roth facility."

"Where does the transport land? In town?" Aurik asked.

"No. About a mile or so from town. You're not thinking of raiding that place, are you?"

Aurik and Sarah looked at each other.

"More of scouting it out right now," Aurik said.

"You guys didn't waste a day getting this revolution thing going, did you?"

"I guess not," Sarah said.

"Thanks, Benjamin," Aurik said. Benjamin nodded.

"One last thing. Which direction from town is this landing site?" Aurik asked as he and Sarah stood.

"North." Aurik nodded a thank you, and Sarah smiled as the two left the barn.

***

Jessica went to work almost immediately when she returned to the cave. She recruited Kyle for the boring task of holding the flashlight while she and Yin worked on connecting one of the power supplies to a salvaged light panel from the shuttle they crash-landed in.

Jessica created a crude power interface, connecting the bare wiring from the small cylindrical power supply to the wiring of the light panel. For safety, she had Yin saw off a salvaged conduit casing to cover the open wires.

The wiring was very similar to what she had been familiar with before she and her squad were put in stasis. It was much like the wiring of the human technology of her time. It consisted of a conduit that the hot wires, or in the case of N'Roth technology hot conductive material, was placed in. She didn't know what the material was exactly, but the wiring felt more like plastic veins than wires but was frayed at the ends just like wires. From what she understood, one could simply connect a few of the frayed ends of the veins to new veins with no degradation of power. The one danger that she knew was that if metal touched these veins, the power would build up until the metal destructively released the buildup of power. This was the method she used when sabotaging the power generator in town.

"Okay, let's see if this works," Jessica said after securing the conduit casing. She stood up and connected another set of veins, careful not to touch the bare tips. The light panel lit up with a hum.

"Okay," she said as she carefully secured another conduit casing around the exposed vein. "We have light now, at least for a while. The light panel shouldn't be drawing too much power, so it'll be a while before we'll need a new power supply for it," she said.

"Now that I have light, I can do the rest pretty much by myself. I'll call for you if I need you."

"Ya don't have to tell me twice. Ya'll wanna come check out this room I found in here? I think Yall'll like it," Kyle said.

"I'm going to try and see if I can hook up this light panel to one of these consoles. I'll check it out later," Jessica replied.

Kyle turned to Yin.

"Sure, I'll go take a look at it," Yin said.

"Yer in for a real treat," Kyle said. "Come on."

***

Jessica started working on one of the salvaged consoles next. They had gutted all of the consoles and dismantled them to transport them to the cave. The frame for the first console was separated into two halves with the panel display into three parts, more than half of the display itself was destroyed during the crash. The wiring and circuit boards for the console were sitting in another pile.

She began filing through the circuit boards, investigating each. Like the power supply, she was familiar with the technology; however, there were significant changes to the N'Roth technology since she left for their mission two-hundred years ago, so she had gaps in her knowledge of the technology.

She picked a couple of circuit boards, set them aside, and found several bundles of the N'Roth vein wiring that she figured would do the job.

Once she gathered all her needed pieces, she began working on a crude splicing of the wires. She decided that she would have to re-visit these projects when she had the proper tools, but for now, she would have to do the best she could.

***

Kyle led Yin through the maze of tunnels and cavern openings that he had mapped out until they reached the large room he had told her about.

They rounded the corner into the cavern, and though the darkness hinted that there would be sunlight as they neared the massive room, her eyes were blinded by the onslaught of light.

The ceiling above contained half a dozen holes of varying sizes that shone with brilliance in the dark cavern, and the rays broke the darkness in beams, illuminating the cavern floor like spotlights shining down on them. Yin gasped in amazement at the sight.

"Wow," she said. "This is amazing."

"I was thinking we could catch rainwater through those holes," Kyle explained.

Yin walked to the center of the cavern, stepping over rock debris and skirting fallen mounds of rock.

"This is the largest room I have found so far," Kyle said.

"What do you think caused all of those holes?" Yin asked.

"I don't know, a storm, maybe, or just time."

"Do you think it's' sa—"

Before Yin could finish her question, a loud boom echoed throughout the cavern, shaking the cave, and the ceiling collapsed.

7

Aurik and Sarah finally neared the transport site. They had discovered the road that led to the compound and followed it through the forest, keeping to the cover of the trees, just in case the road had travelers. The forest on this part of the planet was far less dense and much easier to traverse but also gave less cover; that wasn't an issue as they didn't come across any travelers during their trek.

As they neared the landing site, the terrain opened up into an open field. They slowed and crept low to the ground until they neared close enough to get a good look at the facility.

It was a simple design, and it seemed to have little security. It wasn't fenced or walled, and there stood only a single massive, one-story building at the far side. The shuttle landing pad was a gigantic concrete slab with large boxes and crates neatly stacked in several locations around the pad.

"Aurik, look." Sarah pointed. Aurik followed her finger to a vehicle parked near one of the stacks with a lone man transferring the crates and boxes to it.

"Is that who I think it is?" Aurik asked.

"He did say he keeps busy," Sarah replied. "Looks like he's re-stocking his transport." Aurik nodded.

"I'm willing to bet those big ones are for the N'Roth," Sarah said.

"Yeah. We need to get our hands on those. Come on," Aurik said, and crouching low began back toward the road. Sarah fell in pace behind him.

They waited for the supply vehicle to begin its way back to the small town and into the tree line before getting into position. Sarah stood in the center of the road waving her hands as the driver neared. The driver stopped a few feet from her, then hopped out of the vehicle as he recognized her.

"What are you doing here? You are not allowed out here. You're going to get yourself into a lot of trouble!" he exclaimed, walking over to her.

"More trouble than you realize," she replied, nodding to the transport. The man spun around and, seeing Aurik in the driver's seat, started back toward the vehicle. Sarah jumped into action, grabbing his arm and pulling it up into his upper back as she brought her other arm around his neck. The driver screamed out in pain.

"What-what are you doing?" he asked.

"We're taking your supplies. Please don't resist."

"What, why?"

"Let's just say we're not going to live like slaves. Sorry about this, but you're not too far from where you came from. You will be fine."

Sarah released her grip on the man's neck and forcefully guided him past his transport vehicle.

"I suggest you get yourself back to that shuttle landing pad," she said, letting go of the man and shoving him forward. He didn't even look back as he raced off.

Sarah spun and jumped into the bed of the supply vehicle, and Aurik sped off. The two didn't dare stay on the road for long and drove the transport through the forest.

The vehicle ran much more smoothly over the rough terrain of the wild forest floor than they expected, and they were only jostled when the transport drove over large obstructions.

They skirted the town, stopping halfway between the town and their make-shift base to hide the stolen equipment, then they doubled back several miles away from the stash before abandoning the vehicle and began their hike back to their base.

They had driven the cargo transport several miles in the opposite direction from the base, making sure to discard the vehicle reasonably close to the landing pad in hopes of misleading the N'Roth to believing they were camped near the pad. Hopefully, the N'Roth wouldn't search more than a few miles from the abandoned transport.

Not being familiar with the terrain, they made a point to backtrack as close to the route they had driven the vehicle so they wouldn't get lost.

They finally neared the small city again and, from there, were about to begin their trek back to the base when they noticed a convoy of N'Roth soldiers leaving the city confines.

"That's a lot of soldiers," Sarah said.

"Yeah. Looks like our friend was able to get word out about us," Aurik replied.

They ducked low as the four military convoy vehicles hovered past. The last convoy vehicle stopped, and one of the seven occupants stood up in the bed of the vehicle.

"There's no way they spotted us," Sarah said.

The N'Roth jumped out of the vehicle, glaring into the forest, then barked off orders, and the rest of the soldiers jumped out of their transport and fanned out, disappearing into the forest.

"They know we're here. Come on," Aurik said and spun off, darting into the thick of the forest as quietly as he could. Sarah followed.

They heard N'Roth shouts and knew they had been seen and forsook all attempts at stealth and ran as fast as they could.

***

Kyle heard a snap and felt a surge of pain in his leg as he tumbled to the cavern floor, clumps of ceiling showering down on him, and screamed out in pain.

Then, as sudden as the ceiling had begun collapsing, it was over. Kyle and Yin both lay prone on the cavern floor. Dust swirled around them, making it difficult to breathe, and they couldn't see more than a couple of feet. The bright sun gleamed down through the holes in the ceiling, illuminating the dust and making it just that much more challenging to see past the swirling particles. They almost immediately began coughing.

"Kyle, are you okay?" Yin asked between coughs.

"I think my leg is broken," he replied between coughs, as well. "What about you?"

Yin rolled onto her back.

"Just a few bruises and scrapes. Nothing serious."

Kyle rolled onto his back, screaming out in pain.

"Man, why does this keep happening to me?" he said, grinding his teeth through the pain.

"How bad is it, Kyle?" Yin asked, crawling over to him.

"Well, it probably feels worse than it looks, but man it hurts."

"Don't move. When all this dust clears, we'll get out of here."

"Yin," Kyle said gravely. Yin looked at him, sensing his seriousness. "I don't think we're gonna get outta here very soon." He nodded straight ahead. "That's the way back."

Yin looked in the direction he nodded. The dust had started settling a little, and she could see to the entryway they had come through. It was completely blocked by fallen rocks.

"We can dig our way through the rocks, or we can find another connecting tunnel," Yin said.

"Well, I ain't gonna be much help in digging through that pile of rocks, and it'll be slow goin', me tryin to explore those other tunnels, if they're not caved in, too," Kyle replied.

***

Aurik and Sarah raced through the dense forest with the N'Roth in pursuit. They were running out of breath and knew it was only a matter of time before the seven N'Roth soldiers caught up to them.

It didn't seem to matter which way they turned, the N'Roth still followed, and they knew that, somehow, they were being tracked.

"We can't keep running like this," Sarah finally said as she stopped to lean against a tree.

"You're right. We have to make a stand," he replied.

"The element of surprise is out the window; they have to be tracking us somehow," Sarah said.

"It may not be completely out the window; I have an idea. Help me get up into the tree. If we can get a weapon or two from these guys, it might level the playing field a little."

Sarah gave Aurik a leg to stand on as he climbed up into the tree.

"Quick," he said, as he perched between two branches right over Sarah, "lay down as if you collapsed in exhaustion."

"That won't be too hard to fake," she said as she sat down against the tree base. "I'm pretty close to that state already." She laid on her side with her back leaning against the tree trunk.

Moments later, the two heard N'Roth shouts, followed by a pair of N'Roth soldiers rushing up to Sarah, their rifles trained on her.

Aurik didn't hesitate; the moment they were within a few feet, he dove.

Both soldiers were taken by surprise, and though Aurik tried to knock them both off balance, he only knocked the furthest N'Roth back a step. However, the bulk of his weight hit the other, and the two went tumbling to the forest floor.

***

Sarah took advantage of the distraction Aurik gave and rolled toward the soldier left standing, swiping its legs out from under it. It fell to its back, and with lightning speed, she didn't know she had, Sarah leaped to her knees and dove onto her opponent, grabbing its riffle.

The N'Roth recovered quickly, overpowering Sarah as she took hold of its weapon. Knowing she was about to lose her advantage, she made a desperate attempt to regain the upper hand. Letting go of the rifle, she brought an elbow into her foe's face, adding her entire body weight behind this last-ditch effort to regain control, knowing that if she failed to knock it out or to distract it from focusing on the rifle, she wouldn't live to see another minute.

Her elbow contacted with a painful crack, and the N'Roth went limp. She saw movement to her side. Ignoring the pain, she snatched up the rifle and rolled to her back, firing her weapon into the chest of an advancing soldier.

***

Aurik grabbed hold of the N'Roth's rifle as the two tumbled to the ground, and before the soldier knew what had happened, Aurik had a firm grip of its weapon and ripped the weapon from the N'Roth's grasp as the two rolled. Seconds later, the N'Roth lay dead, and Aurik spun just in time to dodge a rifle blast from another soldier. That soldier and the next fell dead shortly after with an energy blast to their chests.

Aurik saw the next two soldiers emerge from the thick brush and fired. Both dodged the energy bolts, disappearing back into the cover of the forest. Aurik quickly took cover behind a tree. His decision saved his life as an onslaught of energy blasts pummeled the ground where he had been only a second before, following him to the tree.

Smoldering splinters flew through the air as the energy bolts struck the tree, filling Aurik's nostrils with a scent similar to cedar. He dared not return fire yet as the bombardment of energy blasts continued. He couldn't leave the cover of the tree, and he couldn't fire back without getting shot, and he feared that the two N'Roth were biding time. Then, he saw the N'Roth jump out from the brush behind Sarah. Then, he saw an energy blast hit it square in the chest and saw it fall to its back.

The onslaught of energy blasts shifted to Sarah, and she rolled to take cover behind another tree but not before an energy bolt hit her in the side, and she screamed out in pain.

Aurik took advantage of the N'Roth's new focus, disappearing into the thick brush a few feet away, ignoring Sarah's scream of agony.

8

Yin slowly stood to her feet, stretching away the soreness from the onslaught of rocks. She could already feel the bruises forming throughout her body where the ceiling fragments had pummeled her.

"I'm going to see if I can get that entryway cleared," she said, staring at the massive rock barrier in concern. Kyle could hear just a hint of fear in her voice, though she tried to mask her fear in a façade of confidence and started throwing the smaller rocks from the pile over her shoulder.

Yin worked quickly at first, just tossing the loose rocks over her shoulder with no real concern where they landed, but as her muscles began to ache from both the bruising of the cave in, as well as her constant movements, she began to work slower, allowing her doubt to creep into her actions as she began yanking at the more secured rocks, sending small clouds of dust into the air as she pulled and jerked away the rocks.

Kyle tried to lay as still as he could to keep the shooting pain from surging through his broken leg. As he watched Yin work her way through the barrier, he could see her doubts become more and more visible as she steadily worked at clearing the debris. He tried to stand up, leaning a hand on the cavern wall for support to crawl to his feet, but an explosion of pain brought him back to the ground with a thump. He silently cried out, not wanting to distract Yin with concern for him. He was no stranger to pain, but it was then that he knew his leg was hurt badly. If he needed to, he could get up and help, but he decided that he would do that only as a last resort.

It wasn't long before Yin filed through the smaller, easier rocks and graduated to lifting the heavier boulders, tiring her soon after beginning the larger sized masses.

She was just about to give up when she thought she heard something beyond the barrier of fallen debris.

***

Jessica sat on her makeshift chair, working on jerry-rigging more lights when she heard a loud boom, then rumbling, and thought, for a moment, she heard a faint scream.

She paused, strained her ears to listen for the scream, but she heard nothing. The rumbling lasted only seconds, and she heard only silence.

She had never noticed how creepy the silence was before, but as she sat in the quiet listening, it felt eerie. As she sat there listening in the stillness, she began to hear the clattering of crawling things that she had never noticed before. She felt utterly alone for the first time in the giant cave. She could almost feel tiny eyes staring at her in the darkness beyond.

"Kyle, Yin!" she yelled, cutting through the quiet as her voice echoed through the cave, bringing with it a sense of comfort from the silence.

She waited for the echo to subside and listened for a response. After a long moment of nothing, she began to worry.

"Kyle, Yin, are you okay?" she hollered again.

She stood, snatched up a nearby flashlight, and headed in the direction she saw Kyle and Yin go earlier.

She ambled, shone her flashlight beam down every tunnel, and scanned every open room for any sign of her friends.

Her search was slow going as the only light came from her flashlight, which made visibility next to nothing and scanning the cave a tedious task. The cave had dozens, if not hundreds, of alcoves and small rooms, as well as adjoining tunnels that made it difficult to keep her bearings, and she knew if Kyle had not marked the tunnel systems as he did, she would quickly get lost.

She finally came to a tunnel that appeared to have a new cave in as a lot of dust floated among the rocks. She scanned down the tunnel further with her flashlight then turned back to the caved-in section. She slapped hard at the rock, hoping to signal to Kyle and Yin that she had found them—if they were even behind the rock pile—but only succeeded in bruising her palm.

"Kyle, Yin!" she yelled as she rubbed her palm.

"Kyle, Yin! Are you in there?" She pressed an ear to the rocks

to listen for any signs that her friends were on the other side. A

shout, a vibration, a movement of the debris, anything.

A few moments later, she turned to leave, but just as

she turned, she thought she heard a muffled noise coming from

beyond the rock pile.

She turned back.

"Kyle, Yin, is that you?" she hollered.

***

Aurik fell to his back the second he disappeared into the

brush and brought his alien rifle up. He ignored the jarring in

his lungs and back and awkwardly held the alien rifle, grasping

the trigger inside the notch meant for the N'Roth's pincher-like

fingers. A split second later, the pursuer he had suspected

would be chasing him came into view.

The N'Roth felt the blast to the chest before it even saw

Aurik. The soldier fell backward, dead.

***

Sarah buried her face into the forest floor, her side feeling as if a thousand red-hot needles were stabbing into her. She screamed out again.

She didn't notice the N'Roth casually walk up beside her, her mind flushed with a pain she had never felt before. She couldn't concentrate, and she fought to stay conscious.

She had no idea how close she came to death at that moment before the N'Roth spun, hearing its counterpart scream out its final breath.

She heard the energy blasts of a firefight, but she was in too much pain to care. Then she felt a strong hand lift her.

"Sarah," Aurik said, lifting her to her feet. "Sarah, look at me. Focus," he said.

Sarah fought through the pain and threatening blackness and looked up at him.

"We have to move," Aurik said with urgency. "Come on." He wrapped an arm around her. She screamed in agony but allowed Aurik to guide her, every step, every motion sending riveting pain through her body.

The two traveled slowly, making little headway over the next half hour when Aurik noticed beeping from a device that he held in the hand he was using to keep Sarah upright with.

"What is that?" Sarah asked through tired, pain-felt breaths.

Aurik glanced at it, noticing four dots at the edge of the screen. With his other hand, he lifted the alien rifle and tucked its stock under his arm.

"One of the N'Roth had it. I grabbed it before getting you. I think it's how they were tracking us."

"Ah," Sarah replied.

Just as Aurik was about to tell her that the N'Roth found them again, the device screen started fluttering and filling with static.

"What the?" he exclaimed.

"I'm going to set you down for a minute," he said and gently lowered her to the ground.

He backtracked several feet the way they had come, then returned, and passed by Sarah several feet.

"Okay!" he said excitedly. "Come on." He bent low to pull Sarah to her feet, and she screamed out in agony.

Aurik ignored her screaming and hurriedly half carried, half dragged her, not bothering to concern himself with her comfort any longer.

***

Yin dug her face into a cleft in the barrier she had made by removing fallen boulders.

"Jessica!" she hollered and waited for a response.

Yin could barely make out the muffled words, but the distorted sound of her friend's voice gave her a renewed strength, and she began pulling more heavy, small boulders from the barrier. With every moved rock, Yin yelled through the debris in the hopes that she had removed enough of the wall to allow clearer communication. It wasn't long before the faint, muffled screams became more discernable, and finally, the two could make out each other's words.

"Jessica!" Yin hollered.

"Yin!" replied Jessica. "Are you guys okay?"

"Yes, we are okay. Kyle is hurt, but he is doing good."

"Okay. I'll keep digging from my end, and you keep digging from your side."

"Okay," Yin replied and immediately started moving rocks again.

After an exhausting half-hour, the two had removed enough rocks that they had opened a small hole where two large rocks rested beside each other. Yin peered through the opening to see Jessica reaching a hand through. She reached her own hand through, and the two grabbed hands tightly then pulled their arms back out of the small opening.

"It's good to see you," Yin said as she peered back into the hole.

"You too, Yin," Jessica replied. "I can't move anymore on my side. The rocks are too heavy."

Yin nodded.

"Okay. I'll try and see if I can get through on this side."

Jessica nodded, and Yin started moving more of the larger boulders. They were heavier and bigger now, and Yin had to push or pull with exhausting power to budge them from their homes. With every rock she moved now, the mound shifted dangerously.

As Yin began pushing on a wedged rock the size of her head, the debris mound shifted, and a loose section of the ceiling above her fell, pummeling her with more rocks.

She screamed out in pain and surprise, half falling and half running out from beneath the section of collapsing ceiling.

***

Jessica waited long minutes before she saw the small opening grow larger. The two rocks had shifted as Yin removed more debris from the rock mound.

Dust was continually falling from the barrier now as Yin worked to free herself, and every once in awhile, another rock shifted, and the opening grew slightly.

Then, after another several long minutes, the dust fell in a sheet, and she heard rumbling from the other side of the barrier, along with Yin's scream.

She instinctively backed away as the dust filled the chamber, and she began coughing uncontrollably; the dust blinded her from seeing more than a foot or two ahead.

"Yin!" she screamed between coughs.

Yin didn't answer.

"Yin!" she yelled again, panic creeping through her voice.

"I'm okay," Yin said finally.

"What happened?" she asked.

"I caused another cave in when I moved the last rock."

Jessica neared the mound again, scanning it with her flashlight.

"Well, it looks like you opened a bunch more holes, but the top does look more caved in than before."

She peered into the opening again. It had doubled in size, but it was still not large enough to crawl through.

"I don't think we're going to be able to get through this way," Yin said. "One of the tunnels on this side wasn't caved in. We'll try and see if we can find a way out that way."

Jessica nodded.

"Okay, I'll go back and get the medical kit and see if I can find a way to you through the tunnels that we haven't mapped out yet on that side too. Make sure you mark the way you go so you don't get lost."

Yin nodded, and the two grasped hands again through the opening.

"Good luck," Jessica said.

"You too," Yin replied.

***

Aurik practically dragged Sarah through the forest as she constantly screamed out in pain. He could tell from the device in his hand that the N'Roth were gaining on them.

The device kept blinking in and out now, along with a steady flickering, and the static had gotten worse, which confirmed his theory that something was interfering with the machine. He just had to find what it was. It was their only hope of escaping their pursuers.

The device suddenly flickered to complete static. Aurik knew whatever it was that was interfering with the tracker was close. He scanned the horizon in front of him, noticing a cliff a few feet away. He rushed over to the side, peering down.

The cliff bottom was several dozen feet below with a dried riverbed containing some type of rock that he had never seen before. It looked somewhat metallic but sparkled almost like diamonds.

He knew they couldn't get down to the river bed from where they were. He looked at the device; it was still inoperative. The rocks, somehow, were interfering with the signal.

They would just have to follow the cliff edge and hope that they could stay close enough to the riverbed to keep the scanners from working correctly.

He hurriedly pulled Sarah, following the edge of the cliff.

9

Yin helped Kyle to his feet, who groaned as his leg surged with pain at every movement. It took his all not to express his agony more, but he didn't want to worry Yin.

She brought an arm around his back as he rested his over her shoulder to steady himself.

They moved slowly, Kyle limping significantly and leaning on Yin heavily as they snailed their way through the dark, dank cave. Both continuously scanned the cave tunnel with their flashlights they held in their free hands, and within minutes, slow-moving as they were, they had moved beyond the illumination from the chamber that had caved in. They inched their way in darkness again—the only light the two beams from their flashlights.

Kyle was now sweating from the constant strain, and he groaned with every step. Every so often, Yin would stop and dig a deep arrow into the floor of the tunnel, identifying that they had already been there just in case they got turned around.

The tunnel finally split in two directions, and Yin turned down the tunnel that she hoped took them closer to the parts of the labyrinth that they had already explored, near the entrance of the cave. Of course, it was impossible to be sure, not only because keeping a sense of direction in the belly of the planet was next to impossible but also the tunnel they had taken seemed to have wound every which way.

They kept snailing along, and more and more often, Kyle requested a few minutes of rest. Yin knew he was in much more pain than he let on; otherwise, he wouldn't be sweating as much. She was getting thirsty, and she knew Kyle had to be even thirstier.

They had been walking a while now but had no idea how long, nor did they know how much ground they had covered, but they knew it wasn't near as far as they would have liked. With all of the constant resting breaks and moving so slowly, they knew they hadn't traveled far.

After a couple of minutes, Yin pulled Kyle back to his feet and continued through the labyrinth. Minutes later, they came to another split in the cave tunnel. This time, it was three tunnels.

"Oh great," Yin said frustratedly, staring at the three options before them.

"Kyle, you rest here while I scout these three tunnels out," she said at last, then gently helped Kyle to the cavern floor.

"I ain't gonna complain about that," he replied as he sat, breathing heavily through his pain and groaning.

"I'll be back in a minute," Yin said and disappeared into the leftmost entrance.

Kyle sat in the darkness and flipped off his flashlight, allowing the blackness surrounding him to rush in.

He leaned back against the cave wall, listening to the silence. He didn't have to close his eyes as it was utterly dark, but he did anyway, more so because of the pain rather than anything else. He cringed and groaned as he sat there in the blackness, and on occasion, he heard the scuttling of some creature or another, and when he opened his eyes to look toward the sounds, he couldn't even tell his eyes were open except for feeling the blinking of his eyelids.

Sometimes, he would shine his flashlight in the direction of the noises only to reveal rock and dirt.

After several minutes, Yin returned and checked on him before venturing into the next tunnel. A few minutes later, she returned and again checked on him before disappearing into the last tunnel, and just a few minutes later, Yin returned, breathing heavily.

"Come on!" she said excitedly. "I've got to show you something!" she reported, letting her accent bleed through heavier than usual, and she practically yanked Kyle to his feet in her excitement, causing him to scream out. She apologized, gently brought her arm under his, and guided him into the last tunnel.

"What is it?" Kyle asked.

"You will see," she replied excitedly.

***

Jessica returned to the front chamber of the cavern, where she had been working on the lighting and grabbed the N'Roth medical kit Benjamin had provided for them. She snatched up several containers of water, again that Benjamin had provided, and headed into the far chambers that had not yet been explored.

She found the furthest tunnel and headed down it, every so often digging a deep arrow into the ground. She made her way quickly, marking every split she took with a fresh arrow in the cavern floor. She knew just taking random tunnels was not wise, so she always kept to the leftmost tunnels, reasoning that it would be easiest to backtrack.

She found several dead ends and had to backtrack, making sure to scrape a 'D' into the dirt next to the arrows as she backtracked.

She didn't know how long she ventured through the maze of tunnels before she came across another split; this time, however, as she turned down the leftmost tunnel, she noticed a faint light. She picked up her pace, hoping it was Yin and Kyles's flashlights.

"Yin, Kyle!" she yelled as she followed the light. "Is that you?"

***

Aurik pulled Sarah more than helped her along the edge of the cliff. He ignored her screams of agony, hoping the N'Roth nearing wouldn't hear her until he finally turned to her.

"Sarah, I'm sorry, but you have to be quiet."

Sarah didn't acknowledge him, but her screams of agony turned into low squeals of pain as she fought hard to be silent through the torment.

Aurik frantically scanned the cliffside, searching for a way down. They had to get out of sight before the N'Roth saw them. He had no idea how close they were now as the sensor device stopped working due to the mineral formation on the dried-up riverbed.

The cliff morphed into a steep slope rather than a sheer cliff, and Aurik decided that they would have to chance climbing down rather than keeping on the edge in the open.

"Sarah, we're going to have to climb down."

She nodded.

Aurik quickly set her on the ground near the edge and climbed down over the side of the steep slope. When he felt that he had a secure foothold, he grabbed Sarah's arm and dragged her to him. She screamed out in agony but cut it short, remembering the N'Roth nearby.

He pulled her to him, wrapping an arm around her side.

Again, she stifled a scream of anguish as he wrapped his arm around her, not caring to avoid her wound, then she went limp.

The sudden release of Sarah's muscles sent him off balance as her body fell heavily onto his. He fought to keep his balance, but his foot slipped. He did succeed, however, to keep a secure hold of Sarah as he fell and slid down the slope.

Aurik managed to bring Sarah's upper body over his, protecting her from the harshness of the rocks. He could feel them digging into his back as he slid. Sarah's arms and legs dangled awkwardly to the side, her legs scraping the rocks beside him, but he was more concerned in protecting her head and trying to keep from turning or rolling as they fell.

Finally, their fall—or slide—slowed, and he maneuvered to catch himself with his feet on a rock, stopping their descent. His back stung with a dozen scrapes and bruises, but he ignored them and scanned the riverbed.

They were still out in the open, but at least they were out of direct sight for the moment.

He stood to his feet and hefted Sarah's limp body over one shoulder, ignoring the sticky warm blood coating his arm from her wound, and charged off as fast as he could down the riverbed. He noticed that it curved up ahead and hoped they could reach the bend before the N'Roth saw them.

To their luck, just around the bend was a cleft between the sloping cliff and two half-buried rocks.

Aurik climbed as far into the cleft as he could and gently laid Sarah down. It was a deep formation, which was good because it gave more cover in the shadows. He noticed as well that it wouldn't be long until night fell. The light was already dimming, which helped to hide them. He only hoped that night would come swiftly this evening.

Aurik turned to Sarah, checking her pulse. She was alive. He looked over the rest of her, noticing no more open wounds other than the blast wound on her side. It was bleeding, but it wasn't flowing. It was seeping; it looked more like a burn or a scab than anything else. The blood seeped out slowly like a bad burn would, which Aurik thought made sense that if it were an energy blast of some kind—that it would scorch its victims. This wound looked much worse than Kyle's had been, and he knew that Sarah needed medical attention.

He had to do something to help her, but he didn't even know where to begin.

Sarah woke up then with a deep breath of shock, and Aurik slapped a hand over her mouth before she could scream out in pain.

He held a finger to his mouth.

Sarah nodded in understanding.

"We'll get through this, Sarah," Aurik said as he removed his hand. "I know you're in pain, just lie still."

"Where..." Sarah began, fighting for words through her anguish.

"We're hidden. It'll be night soon, and I'll see if I can get to Benjamin's to get a medkit to help you with the pain."

Sarah nodded.

***

Jessica soon realized the light wasn't from her counterparts' flashlights but another entrance to the cave. The closer she got to the light, the more the tunnel lit up, which wouldn't happen with the flashlights she knew.

Soon enough, she was standing in a large, open cavern leading outside.

The cave entrance opened up into a large, crystal-clear lake that looked as though it spanned at least a mile.

She noticed Kyle and Yin sitting at the edge of the entrance near the water.

"Kyle, Yin!" she hollered with glee.

The two turned their heads, and Yin rushed over to her.

"Isn't it magnificent?" Yin asked. "Oh!" Yin snatched the medical kit from Jessica and rushed back to Kyle.

"It sure is," Jessica replied under her breath and headed over to her friends.

Though his leg was still broken, Kyle soon felt much better due to the N'Roth painkilling drugs, and so he could enjoy the view just a little more before they began their slow trek back into the shelter of the cave.

"Ya know," he said, "someone's gonna have to keep an eye on this entrance. Just in case the N'Roth start lookin' for us."

"We'll figure that out later. Right now, we need to get you back into the cave, and when Sarah gets here, we can fix you," Yin said.

"Let's just sit for a while and enjoy the view," Kyle said.

Yin and Jessica agreed, and the three sat watching the sunset and the stars sparkling into existence in the darkening sky.

"Sarah and Aurik should be back by now and are probably getting worried we aren't back in the main chamber. We should get going," Jessica said. Kyle and Yin both agreed, and the three slowly made their way back to the main chamber.

***

"I'll bet Kyle and the others are getting a bit worried that we aren't back yet," Aurik said. "I'm willing to bet the N'Roth have given up by now. I'm going to try to make it to Benjamin's and get a medical kit to help you feel better."

Sarah nodded, and Aurik climbed out from the safety of the crevice, disappearing into the night.

10

Sarah, Jessica, and Kyle reached the main chamber they had been using as their living quarters, noticing that Sarah and Aurik had not returned.

Yin and Jessica helped Kyle to his sleeping bag.

"Try not to move too much, Kyle," Yin said, resting a hand on his arm.

"I ain't gonna argue there," Kyle replied. "Where ya'll think Sarah and Aurik are?"

"I'm sure they are just taking longer than they had planned to get back," Jessica replied. "They'll probably show up here any minute."

"Well, I'm going to get some fresh air for a minute," Yin said and climbed out of the cavern. Once out of the cleft, she climbed on top of the crevice and stared up into the night sky, noticing for the first time since they had crashed on the planet how magnificent it was.

The night sky had an almost iridescent streak of green, pink, and blue that shimmered, spanning a third of the sky.

She wished that she could see more, but the surrounding trees impaired her vision.

Her mind raced every which way with thoughts of war, their failed mission, their new circumstances, and more.

She wondered what it would be like to settle down, have a family, live without war. Most of her adult life was filled with war. She joined the military as soon as she could and never looked back until now. Kyle had been injured, maybe even gravely injured twice in almost as many days, and she found herself thinking less of him as a fellow soldier and more as, well, as someone she wouldn't want to live without.

She could never tell him that, though, and she couldn't bear not to tell him, so she buried her feelings as best she could. She thought of him in pain, and wished she could take it away, take his pain for him.

"Hey," Jessica said, popping up from the crevice. "What you thinking?"

"That Sarah and Aurik should be back by now," she lied. Jessica climbed up to sit by her.

"Beautiful, isn't it?" Yin asked.

"Sure is."

"How's Kyle?"

"He's trying to get some sleep, but he's still in pain as much as the N'Roth painkillers are helping."

Yin nodded.

"What do you think about Aurik and Sarah?" Jessica asked.

Yin thought a moment.

"It's probably not wise to go look for them tonight, especially if they are just late. If they're not back in the morning, I think we should head to Benjamin's, the town, or that landing pad Aurik was talking about to see if we can find them or hear any news about them."

"That's probably not wise either, but I agree, we need to find them if they aren't back by morning. My mind is already racing with the worst-case scenarios," Jessica said.

"Have we done anything wise since crashing on this planet?" Yin asked.

"Good point," Jessica replied.

Yin looked at Jessica.

"But playing it safe never wins wars," she added.

"I'm going to try and get some sleep and try NOT to worry about Aurik and Sarah," Jessica said.

Yin nodded a goodnight, and Jessica climbed back into the shelter of the cave.

Yin stayed sitting on the crevice for a long while, drifting back into her thoughts of Kyle, her friends, old life, new life, and what caused the cave-in in the first place. Then, she finally turned in for the night herself.

***

Aurik moved slower than he would have liked to, but he moved intentionally, keeping his attention on the tracking device he acquired from the N'Roth. He paused regularly to observe his surroundings and take account of his location. He wasn't sure of his exact position but knew he was heading in the general direction towards Benjamin's farm.

Finally, after long hours of moving slowly in the low light of the dense forest, he found the road that led from the small town to Benjamin's farm and followed the road to Benjamin's.

It was late, and the moon was high overhead, so he figured that it would be safe to travel along the road, understanding that it was highly unlikely that he would run into anyone in the middle of the night, but he still kept a close eye on the life-sign detector, just in case.

He saw the farm soon after following the road, and as he neared, he glanced down at the life-sign detector, noticing only a single dot. It was Benjamin, he knew, and as he had suspected, there was not another soul out.

He quickly made his way to Benjamin's cabin and banged on the door.

"Benjamin!" he yelled. "Benjamin, it's Aurik. I need your help."

The door cracked open, revealing a groggy Benjamin, wiping his eyes.

"Benjamin, I'm sorry to wake you in the middle of the night, but I need a medical kit. Sarah's hurt bad."

Benjamin waved for him to enter and took a medical kit from his kitchen.

"What happened to the one I gave you?" he asked, handing the kit to Aurik.

"We aren't at the cave. Sarah and I went scouting that landing pad and ran into some trouble. She got shot by one of the N'Roth rifles."

"Let me get dressed. I'll come with you," Benjamin said and rushed into his bedroom.

"How bad is it?" he asked across the cabin.

"She was shot in the side; it's seeping blood. I wrapped it to try and stop the bleeding."

"That's not going to help; she won't stop bleeding unless we use the N'Roth med kit."

"I was afraid of that."

Benjamin snatched up another kit from his kitchen on his way out. "Just in case," he said and gestured for the door. "After you."

Aurik began the trek back to the riverbed.

"We took shelter in a dry riverbed a few miles from here," Aurik informed.

"I know the place; it goes for miles," Benjamin replied, taking the lead.

"The minerals in the rocks keep the N'Roth tracking devices from tracking for some reason."

Benjamin stopped.

"They're tracking you?"

"Not anymore." Aurik held up the detector. "I took this from one of the N'Roth that was tracking us."

"You killed them?"

Aurik nodded.

Benjamin turned around. "Come on."

The two walked in silence a few minutes before Benjamin spoke up.

"You have gotten yourselves into more trouble than you know. You are not equipped to take on this war of yours."

Aurik didn't reply.

"So far, you have been lucky: Kyle's shoulder was merely grazed, and Sarah's side, from the sound of it, was hit worse. If those blasts had hit with full force, then they both would be dead."

"We will be more careful, and hopefully, the shipment that we stole from the landing pad will have some useful supplies in it," Aurik replied.

Again, Benjamin stopped and stared at Aurik.

"You *stole* a shipment? No wonder they were looking for you." He turned back around. "You certainly are jumping headlong into this revolution of yours," he said as he continued leading the way to the riverbed.

The return trip took much less time due to Benjamin's superior knowledge of the area. Once they reached the riverbed, Aurik led Benjamin to the large cleft.

Sarah woke with a start as the two climbed in.

"Took you long enough," she said. "What, did you decide to stop for dinner?"

"And breakfast," Aurik replied.

Benjamin, understanding the seriousness of her wound, and in no mood to joke, ignored the jesting.

"Turn her onto her side," he ordered.

Aurik obeyed and followed the rest of Benjamin's instructions, Sarah passing out the moment Aurik lifted her.

When she awoke, she felt much better. Her side still hurt unbearably, but compared to what it had been, she didn't complain. Aurik and Benjamin turned their attention to her the moment she woke up.

"How are you feeling?" Benjamin asked.

"Much better. My side is still excruciating, but I can manage."

The two nodded.

"We applied the N'Roth healing compound and wrapped your wound, but it will be several days before you will be fully healed. Try not to get shot again," Benjamin said.

"Will do," Sarah replied.

"It will be dawn soon; I need to start heading back," Benjamin said.

"Thanks again, Benjamin," Aurik said, and Benjamin nodded then looked at the two of them.

"I sure hope you all know what you are doing."

"So do we," Aurik replied.

Benjamin climbed out into the night and began his hike back to his home.

"Are you feeling up to trying to make it back to the cave?" Aurik asked.

Sarah nodded.

"Okay." Aurik climbed out of hiding and waited for the slow-moving Sarah to climb out gingerly, then he wrapped an arm around her, helping her walk, and they began the rest of the trek to the cave.

***

Benjamin neared his farm just as dawn approached. At first, he didn't notice the four N'Roth soldiers at his cabin, nor did he see his employee with them.

By the time he noticed them, they had already begun walking toward him. He recognized the human with them, and his mind raced with terrible possibilities.

The last time he had seen this particular worker was right before he had told Aurik and Sarah where the landing pad was. Had the man seen the three enter the barn? Did he know who Aurik and Sarah were?

11

Aurik guided Sarah through the dense forest. It was much easier now as Sarah's pain was masked by the N'Roth drugs, and her side had begun the healing process aided by the N'Roth healing paste. Though her pain was still significant, it no longer immobilized her.

They made quick time and soon neared the cave. The morning sun had risen soon after they began their journey back to the cave, which expedited their hike even more, the new light allowing them greater visibility and a swifter pace.

***

Yin and Jessica woke much earlier than Kyle, and the two forewent breakfast, gathering supplies for their search for Aurik and Sarah: water, rations, a medkit, and weapons. They had no idea where to start looking, but after a few minutes of discussion, they decided to start by finding Benjamin and asking if he had any news of their friends. If he hadn't heard anything, then they would go back to town to glean information from anyone they could. Then if all else failed, they would start a search.

They were just about to leave when they heard the sliding of rocks from the entrance, and Aurik appeared.

"Aurik!" they both exclaimed, waking Kyle in the process, who jumped with a grunt then scowled with a groan as he moved his leg.

"I could use some help up here," Aurik said and disappeared back up the cleft.

Both Jessica and Yin followed, expressing their relief at seeing him then stopped short when they saw Sarah.

"What happened?" Jessica asked.

"I'll explain after we get her inside and resting," Aurik replied.

The two instantly jumped to action helping Sarah climb down the entrance with Aurik helping from above.

When they got her into the cave, she noticed Kyle lying on his sleeping bag but waited until she was on her own before speaking.

"What happened to you?" she asked.

"Not much, just broke my leg in a cave in, got lost, and found another entrance to the cave. Just resting now," Kyle said.

"Is he serious?" Sarah asked Jessica, who nodded a yes. Sarah leaned back.

"Well, we're going to have to set it soon," she said.

"We were waiting for you to do that," Jessica said.

"Let her rest a little first, then she can help Kyle," Aurik said. The others nodded. Sarah closed her eyes and quickly fell asleep.

They let Sarah rest while Aurik gave an account of everything that had happened since they parted ways outside the village.

"Well, we have had our own excitement here," Yin reported. "Like Kyle said, there was a cave-in, and we had to find another way back through this maze." She motioned toward the tunnels.

"We found another entrance that leads into a large lake," Jessica added. "I was thinking we could set up some kind of reservoir system, you know, for drinking and bathing water."

"Ya'll, we need to find out what caused that cave in," Kyle said. "It happened fast, but it sounded—and felt—like an explosion of some kind that caused it."

They all nodded in agreement.

"Okay," Aurik said. "First, we go to get that stash before it's found. Then when we get back, we'll find out what caused that cave in."

"I'll stay here and look after Kyle and Sarah," Yin said.

"Okay, so Jessica and I will go get the supplies. We'll take the life-sign detector and try to avoid any N'Roth that might be patrolling. Hopefully, they won't have any of the detectors," Aurik said.

"We already have water and supplies prepared. We were about to go search for you," Jessica said.

Aurik nodded and stood. Jessica followed suit, snatching up the packs filled with their supplies, and the two climbed out of the cave.

***

Benjamin sauntered toward the five walking toward him, trying to act casual. His palms were clammy, and his heart raced. His mouth went dry, and he could feel himself sweating already.

He looked over each of the four N'Roth, scrutinizing their demeanors, trying to determine if they were hostile toward him. He even examined the human with them, Jordon; he seemed tense, but then again, he was always anxious around the N'Roth.

Benjamin prepared himself; he was too old to fight and too old to run. If he was discovered as a collaborator with Aurik and his team, then he would just surrender and try to figure out a way to explain himself out of being sent to the prison camp.

"Jordon," he greeted through a dry mouth.

"Benjamin," Jordon greeted.

"Benjamin," said one of the N'Roth Benjamin recognized. "It has been a while since I have come to check up on you," it said.

Benjamin looked over the four N'Roth, glancing at their rifles.

"Ah, don't worry about them," the N'Roth said.

"Well, you have never come here with an armed guard. Is something wrong?" Benjamin replied.

"Yes," the N'Roth replied.

Benjamin's heart skipped a beat, and he hoped no one saw the fear in his eyes or the fact that he gulped down a nervous swallow. He wiped his hands on his pant legs.

"There has been an attack."

Benjamin swallowed again.

"An attack?"

"Yes, several N'Roth were murdered."

"Murdered?"

"Yes," the N'Roth replied coldly, uncaring. "These terrorists are believed to be responsible for an explosion in town."

Benjamin stared, unsure how to react.

"I will be leaving these three here to ensure the safety of your workers."

Benjamin relaxed slightly.

"I see; do you think that is necessary? Are we in danger?"

"That is uncertain, but if these terrorists plan on attacking, we hope to discourage them by increasing security among our investments."

"I see. If you think that is best."

"I do."

Benjamin nodded.

The N'Roth soldier nodded to the other three who left, each taking a different route along the edges of the farm.

The N'Roth turned to leave then turned back.

"Tell me, what were you doing out there?" The N'Roth motioned to the woods where Benjamin had come from.

Benjamin's heart began racing again, and his palms started sweating.

"I was just going for a walk."

"Before dawn, in the dark?"

"I woke up and couldn't get back to sleep, so I thought to take a walk. Clear my mind."

"With a med kit?"

Benjamin looked down at the medkit in his hand. He had forgotten about it.

"Uh, yeah. Just in case I get hurt on my walk. Like you said, it was dark." Benjamin smiled as best he could, hoping it looked innocent and genuine.

"I see. That was wise."

Benjamin nodded a thank you.

"I would refrain from venturing into the woods, especially in the dark for now, until these terrorists are caught."

“Will do. Thank you.”

The N’Roth nodded and left. Benjamin watched him go, relief flowing through him, and he let out a heavy sigh, then he noticed Jordon still standing there staring at him.

“Did you need the medkit today?” Jordon asked as he noticed Benjamin’s attention focusing on him.

“What, no,” Benjamin replied.

“Then who’s blood is that on your boot?”

Benjamin looked down, noticing for the first time Sarah’s blood smeared on his boot. “Oh, that’s probably berry juice from a berry I stepped on.”

“Oh,” Jordan replied, unconvinced, “well, I better get ready to clock the workers in.” He turned and left.

Benjamin made his way to his cabin and plopped down in his living room chair, breathing a massive sigh of relief.

He thought of how he would get word to Aurik about the increase of security and the inevitable search for them.

***

Aurik led Jessica through the forest, keeping clear of the town just in case N'Roth soldiers were patrolling the areas.

They hiked for hours before Aurik stopped and explained that they were close.

He and Sarah had picked an easily identifiable area to hide the shipment so they would be able to find it relatively easy. He found the stash and uncovered the metallic crate.

They opened the crate rather easily. It had no lock but a simple, thick seal with N'Roth writing that warned against unauthorized opening of the seal. It seemed that the N'Roth had no expectation of having their equipment stolen, and so they never bothered to incorporate higher security measures. He imagined that would start to change.

"Whoa, jackpot!" Jessica exclaimed at seeing the contents.

"No kidding," Aurik replied, as he started unloading the crate.

They counted eight N'Roth energy pistols, three rifles, a dozen medkits, another life-sign detector, another half dozen cylindrical power supplies twice the size as the ones they had stolen, a dozen N'Roth knives, and a dozen N'Roth uniforms.

"Okay, well, I say we leave two pistols and a medkit and the life-sign detector in here and hide it really good. We'll keep this as an emergency weapon's stash," Aurik said.

Jessica agreed, and they returned the discussed items back into the crate then stuffed the rest into their packs. They buried the container deep in the ground and set some branches over the fresh dirt, dropped several rocks on the branches, and then added a few more branches.

"Hopefully, that will hide it well enough," Aurik said. "Okay, let's get heading back."

Aurik grabbed his pack and froze as he noticed the faint beeping from the tracking device and the four dots on its screen closing in on them.

12

Aurik and Jessica had been so focused on their new stash and supplies that neither of them had bothered to keep an eye on the life-sign detector.

The four dots were closing fast.

"Grab the rifles," Aurik ordered as he threw on the pack, strapping it tightly, the buttstock of one of the rifles sticking awkwardly out of it.

Jessica, already having her pack on, snatched up the two remaining rifles, handing one to Aurik.

"This way, quick," Aurik ordered and darted off.

***

The two raced through the dense forest, Aurik glancing down at the life-sign detector every few seconds. The N'Roth were still in pursuit and didn't seem to be backing down from the chase.

"We're not losing them. I have an idea," Aurik said. "Follow me."

Aurik led Jessica through the forest toward—he hoped—the dried riverbed that he had found the day before with Sarah.

It was easy to get turned around in this dense forest, and he only hoped that he had been able to keep his sense of direction accurate. If not, he knew they were in trouble.

Two more dots had shown up on the tracker, and he knew the N'Roth had radioed their positions in for reinforcements. Undoubtedly, there would be more N'Roth showing up to corner them in.

To Aurik's relief, just a few minutes later, they ran into the dried riverbed. The forest cleared just before the edge, and they almost ran right over the cliff edge, despite the tracker malfunctions signalizing that they were close to the riverbed; they came upon it so quickly. Luckily, Aurik was able to stop fast enough to keep from falling over the edge, but not before Jessica almost knocked him over it when she bumped into him.

"Come on," Aurik said and backed into the edge of the tree line. "Keep an eye out for any N'Roth," he said as he began along the edge of the tree line. "We're going to follow the tree line as far as the reverbed will keep the life-sign detectors from reaching us."

Jessica nodded.

***

The two followed the tree line under the cover of the trees, making sure to scan the forest for any N'Roth searching for them. They both knew they were far from out of the woods, though. There had to be a score of N'Roth searching parties looking for them, and they were heading the opposite way of their base.

They knew that they couldn't risk leading the N'Roth back to their camp, and so Aurik was leading them in the opposite way in hopes that the N'Roth would confine their searches to the vicinities where they had been spotted and not anywhere else.

They slowed their run to a jog, both to catch their breath and to conserve energy. After a couple of miles, they finally stopped.

"Okay. Here's what I'm thinking," Aurik began. "We cross this riverbed and backtrack to our camp. As long as we stay close enough to the riverbed, we won't show up on the life-sign detectors, plus it is less likely that we will run into N'Roth."

"Okay, sounds good. I want to grab a handful of those rocks to study too. See why they interfere with the sensors."

They heard the rustling of trees just a few feet off, and both fell silent as they dropped to the ground and locked their rifle muzzles in the direction they heard the noise.

Seconds later, three N'Roth soldiers pushed through the brush only to fall dead.

"We need to get moving," Aurik said.

"Agreed," Jessica replied.

The two jumped to their feet and raced along the edge of the tree line again, and after several minutes, they slowed and cautiously emerged from the tree line as they scanned the length of the cliffside for any N'Roth.

They saw none and followed the cliff edge until they found a relatively safe area to climb down and were across the riverbed and in the safety of the trees on the other side in minutes, and they began their trek back toward their camp, keeping their eyes and ears alert.

After several hours, the riverbed curved sharply away from their base. Aurik paused before stepping out from the safety of the tree line, turning to Jessica.

"Okay, the cave should only be a couple miles from here," he said.

"How do you know that?" Jessica asked.

"Benjamin told me last night when we were waiting on Sarah to heal enough to be moved. He told me that the N'Roth diverted the water to some kind of power plant or something."

"Power plant?"

"Yeah, it's miles away. Benjamin said they have a whole other colony that works the plant."

"We have to check it out."

"I was thinking the same thing, but not until everyone is well enough."

Jessica nodded.

"Okay, let's go," Aurik said and rushed out of the tree line, Jessica following close behind.

They climbed down the small cliffside and back up the other side swiftly, returned to the cover of the trees, and continued their way toward their secret base.

After a few minutes, the life-sign detector flickered back online, and Aurik kept a close eye on it as he led Jessica to their hideout.

***

When Aurik and Jessica finally reached the cave, it was well into the afternoon, and they found Sarah awake and moving about the cave and Kyle asleep with a splint made from two tree branches on his leg.

Sarah and Yin immediately noticed them.

"So what did we get?" Sarah asked.

The two replied by tossing the packs to Sarah and Yin. Sarah pulled out the rifle protruding from the pack, and both dumped out the contents onto the cavern floor.

"Whoa," Yin exclaimed.

"You're telling me," Sarah added.

"I take it you are feeling better?" Aurik asked Sarah.

"Still hurts, but nothing I can't manage. This N'Roth healing stuff works wonders, and I took some of the painkillers. Even with all of the N'Roth meds, though, it still hurts, but like I said, nothing I can't handle."

"Looks like you fixed Kyle's leg," Aurik said.

"Yeah. Gave him painkillers too, but he'll have to keep off the leg for a while unless the N'Roth have some kind of miracle bone-mending device," Sarah replied.

"Well, I wouldn't doubt it based on what's in the simple medkits," Jessica said.

"It's going to start getting dark soon, so I'm going to get some much-needed shuteye. In the morning, we'll start making plans to investigate that explosion you were talking about.

The three nodded, and Aurik plopped down on his sleeping bag, falling asleep in seconds.

***

Benjamin had spent the day trying to keep busy and not worry about Aurik's team.

The N'Roth soldiers left to guard the farm stayed closer to the center of the fields rather than the outskirts, and he kept a close eye on them. They patrolled the center fields all day, never once stopping their patrol routes until their relief came, which did the same until the end of the workday.

Benjamin tried not to look nervous or preoccupied when the patrols neared, but he felt as if he was being scrutinized all day. He couldn't shake the feeling that they were watching him, though he never once saw any of the N'Roth look toward him. They patrolled, staring out into the surrounding forest. Still, he couldn't help but shake the feeling.

He eventually shook it off as lingering unease from his morning encounter with the N'Roth.

****

An hour after the workers had all left for the day, in the cover of night, Benjamin left his cabin. He scanned the fields to see if the N'Roth soldiers were still patrolling, and when he was satisfied that they had gone, he rushed into the nearby forest.

He didn't see the shadowy form crouched in the dark near his cabin.

He didn't notice the dark figure follow him into the forest.

13

Benjamin hurried through the forest. He was paying little attention to his surroundings and didn't hear the shadowy figure following him. It wasn't long before he made it to the cleft that led into the cave entrance Aurik and his team were using as a base.

When Benjamin disappeared behind the dense brush that hung low in front of a protruding cleft in the side of the mountain and didn't come back out, the dark figure followed.

***

Benjamin knelt down and shook Aurik awake.

"Benjamin," Aurik said groggily, "what are you doing here?"

"I have some important news to tell you," Benjamin replied.

A light suddenly blinded Benjamin, and he instinctively brought up a hand to block it.

"Benjamin, what's going on?" Sarah asked upon seeing him, lowering her flashlight.

Benjamin looked over, directing his comment to both Aurik and Sarah.

"I have news of the N'Roth," he said, loud enough for both to hear, which woke Kyle and Jessica.

"Benjamin. Is that you?" Kyle asked.

"Yes. I want to warn you all. The N'Roth are sending out search parties for you."

"We know," Jessica replied.

"Oh," Benjamin said. "They have added patrols to the farm."

"Yeah, we figured it was only a matter of time before they started adding more security measures because of us," Aurik said.

"I see," Benjamin replied. "So it was a waste of time, me warning you?"

"Not a waste!" said a voice near the cave entrance.

Jessica jerked her flashlight toward the voice, again blinding her target, who brought a hand up to block the bright light.

Benjamin stood to his feet, realizing that he had been followed.

"Jordon! You followed me?"

"It wasn't hard, Benjamin. You weren't trying to be sneaky."

"What are you going to do?" Benjamin asked.

"Nothing," Jordon began, "but I would appreciate you lowering the light." Jessica lowered the light to the ground.

"Why are you here?" she asked.

"I want to join you." The chamber went silent as the team reflected on what Jordon had said.

"How did you know to follow me?" Benjamin asked.

"And why do you want to join us?" Kyle added.

Jordon turned to Benjamin. "I saw you meeting in the barn and then the blood this morning, and you were nervous all day. I thought that maybe you knew more than you were letting on with the N'Roth." He turned to face Kyle, barely able to see him across the chamber with the meager lighting from the flashlight.

"I *hate* the N'Roth. They killed my brother. *That* is why I want to join you." Jordon's already hard features seemed to grow even harder as he spat the sentence out, and they all could hear the hate in his voice.

After a moment, Aurik spoke up. "Jordon, right?"

"Yes," he replied, turning to face Aurik and Benjamin.

"It's late. We will be in touch. You and Benjamin need to get back before anyone discovers your absences. You live in the town, yes?"

"Yes."

"Good. For now, you will be our eyes and ears. Anything you hear and see report to Benjamin for now. Especially shipments, troop movements, rumors, and new security measures."

Jordon nodded.

"Don't be too nosy. You don't want to seem suspicious."

Again, Jordon nodded.

"Both of you, get going," Aurik ordered.

Benjamin started toward the exit while Jordon began his climb out of the entrance.

"Benjamin," Aurik called as he stood and walked over to him. "Thanks for the warning."

Benjamin nodded.

"Can he be trusted?" Aurik whispered.

"I think so," Benjamin replied, then turned to follow Jordon out.

Once the two were gone, Aurik turned to the others.

"Okay, we're going to take shifts on watch tonight, just in case." They all nodded.

"I'll take the first watch," Jessica said.

"Okay, wake me in about four hours," Aurik ordered. Jessica nodded and grabbed one of the N'Roth riffles, then perched herself at the cleft entrance.

***

Benjamin exited the cave, and once he was through the hanging cover that concealed the opening, he grabbed Jordon's arm, spinning him around.

"Are you sure you know what you are doing?"

"Yes," Jordon replied sharply.

"They can't win. It's only a matter of time before they are caught and killed, along with anyone helping them."

"Does that include you?"

Benjamin dropped his arm, softening his tone.

"I am old. If I get caught, I have lived my life; you have not. Why are you helping them?"

"For the same reason as you are, Benjamin. Hope. Even if they do get caught, you hope they don't, and deep down, you know, despite the chances of failure, there might just be a possibility to be free." Jordon turned back around. "Come on, we have to get back."

Despite Benjamin's doubt in the slightest possibility of this group's success, and despite that Benjamin had little hope that he and his fellow humans would ever be free of the N'Roth control, he cracked a smile.

It had started, and even through all of his hopelessness and doubt, a small spark of hope rose in his core. Jordon was proof that the possibility of success, however unlikely, *could* happen.

***

The next morning Jessica immediately went to work on connecting another console to one of their new power sources. She'd had an idea in the middle of the night on how to make their base more secure.

She was the first awake and had already connected the power supply to the console, like she had with the first, when the others finally stirred, and Aurik returned from keeping watch.

The console blinked to life with a hum, and Jessica scanned the readouts. The writing was N'Roth, as expected, but she could make out most of what the readouts indicated.

She spent the next few minutes scrolling through readouts and settings programmed into the console, taking note of what might be useful and what programs to remove so she could free up space to write her own programming in.

Aurik came up beside her. "What have you found?" he asked.

Jessica looked up.

"Not much, really. Mostly N'Roth shuttle programming. There's some sensor programs and basic shuttle operations we might be able to modify, but most of the programming we can wipe," she replied.

Aurik nodded.

"Well, I set up some tripwires a few feet before the entrance, so we should be warned if anyone gets close.

"Tripwires?"

Aurik held up a few pans that Benjamin had given them and clanged them together.

"If anyone trips them, we will hear," he explained.

"I see. If I can get this console to work like I want it to, then we won't need to be so primitive," Jessica replied.

"What exactly are you wanting to do with this console?"

"I started thinking last night about that life signs detector, then it just came to me. If we can figure out a way to boost that LSD range, then we can know when people are near. I thought with the new power supplies, we might be able to interconnect the console with the LSD and expand the range using the sensor programming in the N'Roth shuttle system."

"Okay. I'll let you get back to it then. I'm going to start breakfast." Jessica nodded and returned to working on the console.

***

Aurik finished the morning meal quickly, which consisted of beans.

"Breakfast is ready," he informed, and Sarah and Yin rushed over.

"I'm starving," Sarah said as she scooped a spoonful into her bowl.

Yin scowled at having to eat beans, but scooped a large spoonful into two bowls, handing one to Kyle as he plopped down beside him. He still lay on the sleeping bag, but he had moved so that his leg sprawled out toward the center of the chamber.

Jessica still worked on the console, ignoring the announcement and the smell of cooked beans wafting through the chamber until Aurik practically had to order her to eat something. She reluctantly joined her counterparts for breakfast.

"We need to start thinking about hunting for food. We are running out of our rations. We have a day, maybe two at most, left," Aurik said.

The others agreed.

"I'm thinking," Sarah said, "that Yin and I can start building a reservoir from that lake we found so it will be easier to get water."

"Sounds good," Aurik replied.

The team finished their meal, discussing goals and plans for the next few days. One of which was for Aurik to meet up with Benjamin and Jordon while the others worked on their respective projects.

***

Aurik knew it was dangerous to venture out in broad daylight now. The past few days testified to that with the N'Roth patrols, which most likely had LSD devices. He, however, didn't. He left it with Jessica so she could get the sensors online. He counted on being able to blend in with Benjamin's workers when he got to the farm. He counted on the LSD not being able to differentiate between individuals with the implanted chip Benjamin had mentioned and those without. He counted on the LSD not being able to identify specific life signs belonging to particular individuals. He counted on the N'Roth focusing their patrols near the areas where they had stolen equipment or had already been seen. He counted on the N'Roth not venturing to this part of the forest.

He counted on a lot, but he needed to talk to Benjamin. They needed supplies. Something was going to go wrong, he knew. Nothing had gone how they had planned since they landed on the planet. They were in over their heads, and they were barely keeping their heads above water. They had been careless from the moment they had woken up from stasis, and he was being careless now. He had a suspicion that his carelessness, like all the other times, would come back to bite him.

14

Aurik met no resistance on his way to Benjamin's but noticed the N'Roth patrol almost immediately. He crouched in the trees watching the patrol for a few minutes and then skirted the farm, keeping in the cover of the tree line until he neared the barn.

It was still quite a walk in the open to the barn, but at least it wasn't as wide open as the rest of the fields. There were a lot of workers, so he knew he would most definitely be spotted. The only other way in that might not be noticed would be from the street leading to the town.

There would undoubtedly be a patrol near that area, but he thought that just walking up through that entrance might be the safest way. He could always claim that he woke up late and missed the transport and had to walk. He hoped that would work.

He followed the tree line to the road and hopped out onto the middle of the thoroughfare.

***

As soon as she had finished eating her breakfast, Jessica went right back to working on the console. She spent the next several hours working on programming in patches to connect the N'Roth life signs detector. It was slow going because she had to write the coding in N'Roth, and though she had learned the language, it was frustratingly difficult for her to program the device.

She made it a point to remember to write a translation program whenever she had the free time—if she ever had the free time.

"Yes!" she exclaimed as she saw the readout pop up on the console's screen. A cluster of small dots stood in the center of the screen. She tapped on the cluster of dots, and the screen zoomed in, revealing four dots.

Two dots were stationary, and two more were moving. Short symbols next to two dots blinked, which Jessica knew as N'Roth numbers, revealing the distance from the center point.

One dot stood in the center, and another stood mere feet away while the two moving dots were dozens of yards farther. She watched as the dots moved closer to the center of the console until they were almost on top of the two stationary dots.

Jessica spun around to see Sarah and Yin entering the cave.

"Good news, guys, I expanded the signal of the life signs detector so we'll be able to know when someone is coming," she said.

The two dropped the branches they were carrying onto a pile they had been gathering and sauntered over to Jessica, brushing their hands clean on their pants.

"The dots are us," Jessica said as the two neared. "Kyle, me, and you two," she said, pointing to each dot.

"How far does it reach?" Sarah asked.

Jessica tapped the screen again, and the display zoomed out into the large view.

"It looks like maybe a hundred yards or more," she replied. "It appears those numbers indicate the distance." She pointed to symbols spread along the top and the right edge of the display screen.

"At least we'll have a minute or two warning," Yin said.

The two nodded.

"I'm going to hook up that last control panel and see what useful programs I might be able to find on it," Jessica said.

"All right. We will get back to gathering more wood," Sarah replied, and Yin and Sarah ventured back outside to gather more wood.

***

Aurik walked right into the farm with no interference. He had stashed his weapons just a few feet into the tree line just in case he was searched. The N'Roth patrol watched him as he made his way down the main road to the farm. Fields stood tall on both sides. One looked like a cornfield, and the other looked like a wheat field. He wondered how many different products were grown at Benjamin's farm.

He hadn't noticed before that there had been more than one thing grown. The N'Roth did have some remarkable technology, so it made sense that they would have agricultural advances as well.

He scanned the fields for Benjamin or Jordon as he walked but did not see them. He was almost to Benjamin's cabin when he saw Jordan near the barn.

Aurik chuckled to himself. The barn, it seemed, was beginning to be the secret meeting place.

Aurik made his way into the barn, making sure to be seen by Jordon, and waited. He didn't have to wait long as Jordon entered just a couple of minutes later.

"Is this going to be a regular thing?" Jordon asked as he entered.

"I hope not," Aurik replied. "We need supplies and to discuss how we can make regular contact with each other."

Jordon thought a moment.

"Okay. Well, we can't keep meeting here in broad daylight," Jordon replied.

"Agreed."

"There's a spot at the edge of the forest by one of the fields that the workers like to take their breaks. We will start meeting there. It's near the road as you come in from town."

Aurik nodded.

"We'll meet in the daytime only if absolutely necessary. I don't want to chance getting caught so easily anymore," Aurik added.

Jordon nodded in agreement.

"I usually leave water out for the workers in the tree line by several large boulders. It's pretty dense around that area. I fill it up around closing time. When I go to fill it up around then, if I see ..." Jordon paused a moment, trying to think of something to signal that they needed to meet. "... I'll leave my thermos there with strips of yellow and red bands around it. When you want to meet that night, leave the yellow band around it and put the red inside. If it is an emergency and can't wait until dark, then put the red band around it and put the yellow band inside. I'll start going there throughout the day as well just to check."

"Sounds good. Yellow to meet that night, red for an emergency meeting."

Jordon nodded.

"Okay, can you get us any of these, by chance?" Aurik handed Jordon a small sheet of paper. Jordon looked it over and nodded.

"Some of the stuff, no problem, but there are a few items here that may be difficult, if I can get them at all, and some of these are restricted to N'Roth. There's no way I can get those."

"Okay, get what you can for us, and welcome to the revolution," Aurik replied.

Jordon smiled, shoving the list deep into his pocket. "Check tonight for your supplies." With that, he left.

***

Jessica soon got the last of the salvaged consoles up and running, connecting it to the same power source that the life signs detector console was connected to.

It was a smaller console that Jessica did not know what it had been used for in the shuttle and practically hollered out as she began reading the display.

It was a communications console, which meant that they might be able to modify it to transmit on a secure line to each other. A few modifications and she could easily code a secure channel. The only problem was they didn't have any communication devices to take advantage of the console.

She noticed something then. A readout that she wasn't expecting.

"What the heck! No way!" she exclaimed. She tapped the display, and it blinked into the next screen. "This can't be," she said under her breath. "There's no way our luck can be *that good*," she said to herself.

***

Aurik waited a few minutes before leaving. Again, he casually made his way through the fields without confrontation. Once he neared the edge of the fields, he scanned to his right for the break area Jordon had mentioned.

"You there!" hollered a scratchy voice. Aurik turned around, trying not to act suspiciously.

"Shouldn't you be in the fields working?" an N'Roth soldier asked as it neared.

"Uh. Yes, sir. Uh. I was told I could take a break," Aurik replied.

"Didn't I just see you come in a few minutes ago? You already need a break?"

"Uh, yes, sir. It's a long walk from town, and I'm not feeling all that well. I was told I could rest a few minutes."

The N'Roth soldier narrowed its eyes. "I see."

"Uh, sir. I'm new here, and they said there was somewhere around here that we could take a break at. Has water."

The N'Roth pointed a few yards down the edge of the field.

"Uh, thank you, sir."

The N'Roth soldier replied with an irritated growl and continued his patrol route. Aurik sighed in relief and made his way to the break area. He made a point to get water and sit down near the edge of the trees in the shade until the N'Roth soldier moved beyond sight then darted into the forest.

He found his weapons stash and began tossing the branches he used to camouflage them when he heard the scratchy voice of another N'Roth behind him.

"What are you doing out here?" it said.

Aurik froze.

"Stand up," it ordered.

15

Aurik stood slowly, pulling the branch he was still holding back over his weapons stash and raised his hands over his head.

"Turn around," the N'Roth ordered.

Aurik slowly turned around, trying to look as terrified as he could.

The N'Roth pointed its rifle up at Aurik's face. Aurik turned his head away, putting his hands up in front of his face.

"No, no!" he said, fainting panic as best he could.

"What are you doing out here?" the soldier asked again.

"I, uh, I was sneaking food," Aurik lied.

"Stealing food?" The N'Roth narrowed its eyes.

Aurik nodded frantically.

Aurik knew that he had to think fast.

"Stand aside," the N'Roth ordered.

Aurik knew the moment that the soldier saw his weapons stash that he was a dead man. He had to think of something and think fast.

"Move aside!" the N'Roth ordered again, shoving its weapon closer to Aurik's face.

This was it. This was Aurik's only chance. Aurik stretched his hands out defensively, closing his eyes in an imitation of fear.

"Okay, okay. Don't shoot," he said.

Aurik knew if the N'Roth got a shot off, even if it didn't hit him, the sound would alert the nearby patrols. He had to disarm the soldier and keep it from notifying the other patrols, which would inevitably come looking for the cause of the disturbance.

In one swift motion, Aurik stepped to the side, grabbing the barrel of the soldier's rifle, forcing the barrel down as he stepped closer, and yanked the rifle away as hard as he could.

The N'Roth, caught off guard at the sudden attack, had no time to react before its rifle was stripped from its pincher-like hands, however, the strap caught around its shoulder, sending it stumbling forward.

Aurik took advantage of the N'Roth's imbalance, bringing a foot into the alien's path and sending it hurtling to the ground and thumping its face into the forest floor.

The N'Roth's fall stripped Aurik of his hold on the rifle, and it thudded to the soft forest floor next to the N'Roth.

The alien soldier instantly reached for the weapon, and Aurik leapt onto its back, grabbing for the rifle as well.

The soldier let out a scratchy scream, and Aurik immediately leaned an elbow into the alien's jaw, pressing as hard as he could, stifling the cry into the soft forest grass.

He leaned as hard as he could on the face of his foe while struggling to keep the N'Roth from regaining hold of its weapon.

The two wrestled for the weapon, the N'Roth squirming to knock Aurik off balance and Aurik desperately trying to keep a heavy elbow on his enemy's jaw to keep it from alerting its counterparts.

The N'Roth shifted its weight, stretching toward the rifle, sending Aurik off balance just enough for the alien to get the upper hand. Aurik had to shift his weight to rebalance himself, which allowed the N'Roth to finally grab the weapon and move even more out from under Aurik's elbow.

The soldier twisted, sensing that Aurik was still off balance, trying to knock Aurik off of him. Aurik caught himself before falling, but not before the soldier was able to grab a better hold of the rifle and shout.

Aurik recovered quickly, seeing the shoulder strap had now fallen to the N'Roth's elbow, he snatched a dangling portion of the strap, stretching it as much as possible as he pulled the strap hard, up and around the soldier's neck.

The soldier, now with its arm trapped around the strap, desperately tried to claw and scratch at Aurik with his pincher appendages, but its arm was being pulled close to its face as Aurik tightened the strap around its neck.

With one hand, Aurik pulled on the strap with all of his might and fended off the alien's free arm with his other hand.

Aurik had a slightly better position than the N'Roth as he still lay on top of the soldier. The alien was forced to reach backward awkwardly to reach Aurik, desperate to find something, anything to grab in hopes of freeing itself.

It tried to scream, but only managed a weak guttural noise, and soon it fell limp. Its arms went still, but Aurik held tightly for a few more seconds before releasing the creature.

Aurik dropped on top of it, breathing heavily from the exhausting battle, then listened quietly for any sounds of approaching soldiers.

When he was finally satisfied that the N'Roth's screams -as short-lived as they were – were not heard, he stood. Still out of breath, he untangled the rifle strap from the dead soldier's limbs and slung the weapon over his back. He then took the N'Roth by the feet and quietly dragged him several dozen yards deeper into the forest, hiding the corpse in thick underbrush.

Aurik knew that it would only be a matter of hours before the body began to stink and a matter of days before it was found, but he hoped the wildlife would devour the N'Roth before it was discovered by other patrolling soldiers.

He returned to his stash and quickly snatched it up, then headed back to base to relay the specifications for contacting Jordon to the rest of his team.

***

Aurik climbed down the entrance to the cave and set the two rifles against the cave wall near the entryway.

"Aurik, come look at this!" Jessica requested.

Aurik sensed the excitement in her voice and rushed over.

"What is it?" he asked.

Jessica tapped on the small console she was standing in front of.

"This console is a communications console, and that icon will connect us to the N'Roth facility." She tapped the icon, and the screen blinked into an N'Roth readout.

"Are you serious?" he exclaimed, resting his palms on the edges of the console. "But wait, there looks like there are two facilities listed."

"Yes, I think this one is the one in the village." She pointed to the top readout. "But the other one, I have no idea what it is. So, with this device, we can hopefully connect to the N'Roth compound and download their files. "

She paused and winced slightly at her coming words.

"But there is a catch."

Aurik looked up at her, furrowing his brow in apprehension.

"What's the catch?"

"If we link up, there is a slight possibility that we can be tracked."

"I see," Aurik replied, removing his hands from the console.

"But," Jessica added, "if we connect at the right time, say when nobody is looking at this particular screen, we could get away with it, and I can write a virus that should erase any traces that we even connected. But if someone just happens to be looking at the right screen at the right time, and notices the connection, then they might be able to find us.”

She looked hopefully at Aurik as he took a few steps away, then turned around.

He considered the potential of being caught, and weighed it with the benefits of connecting to the N’Roth facility. He spoke carefully, but his voice conveyed hints of excitement.

“Well, we haven’t exactly been playing it safe since we woke up from stasis. It’s a risk, but one that I think is worth it. Let’s do it.”

Jessica smiled with glee, clapping her hands together.

“I was hoping you would say that. I’ve already started working on clearing these consoles of everything that we don’t need so we can store the files in our database. When I’m done with that, I’ll start working the antennae we’ll need, then I can create the virus.”

“Great. Let’s just hope we don’t come to regret this.”

Jessica nodded in agreement and returned to deleting the unnecessary files.

"Where's Sarah and Yin?" Aurik asked.

"They're working on creating that aqueduct we discussed. The cave is marked now, so just follow the signs."

"Hmm, great. Thanks."

"Yep."

Aurik had noticed on his way in that Kyle was asleep, so he thought to let him rest and help Yin and Sarah with the aqueduct until they ate again. When they ate their meal, he told them how to contact Jordon, then left again to meet up with him at the farm.

***

It was well after dark when Jessica had finally finished preparing for the file transfer, and they waited until the moon was high in the starry night sky before attempting the connection. Before Aurik had left, he had secured a small antenna to a tree outside the cavern entrance so they could be

sure to get a good signal.

"Okay, let's cross our fingers and hope that nobody will

notice," Jessica said to Sarah, Yin, and Kyle, and she began the

download.

16

Aurik made it to the farm fields with no trouble yet again, and this time found no resistance at the fields either.

He decided to check on the dead N'Roth and found to his liking that it had already been partially devoured by the local wildlife, though it was largely untouched, and he could already smell the stench of the N'Roth's decomposing body.

When he reached the designated meeting spot, he found Jordon waiting just inside the dense tree line, staring out into the open farm fields.

Jordon spun around apprehensively as he heard Aurik approach. He sighed in relief as he realized it was Aurik.

"I thought you were an N'Roth patrol," he said.

"Your first clandestine meeting?"

"My what?"

"Secret. Your first secret meeting?"

"Yes. The N'Roth left a while ago, but still. Anyway, here is what I could get." Jordon brushed away a pile of tree branches next to him, revealing two grain sacks.

"I put them in these so I wouldn't draw too much attention." Aurik nodded.

"Thanks."

"I was able to get several weeks of food from the market. Most of it should last a while. Some of the other supplies you requested are in there too, but I'll have more for you in a couple of days." He handed the two sacks to Aurik. Aurik took the sacks with a nod and turned to leave, then turned back.

"By the way, is there another N'Roth facility on this planet besides the compound?" he asked.

"Yeah, it's a labor camp. Why?"

"Jessica was able to power up a console we salvaged from the shuttle we crashed in, and we noticed there were two separate com designations on the readout."

"You guys have power?" Jordon asked.

"We acquired some power cells," Aurik replied, "and Jessica was able to patch them into a couple consoles from our crashed shuttle."

"Impressive. This revolution of yours just might work. I can't imagine what you could do with an army," Jordan commented.

"What?" Aurik asked.

"Well, it's just the five of you, and you've already managed to create a secret, powered base, gain a couple members to your fight, create an underground supply chain, and upset the N'Roth in just a matter of days. Imagine what you could do with an army." Jordon said.

"You mean like an army of freed labor camp workers?" Aurik suggested with a grin.

Jordon looked at Aurik in shock.

"What? No. I just meant that you could probably accomplish a lot more if you had more people on your side! I didn't suggest to attack the labor camp!"

"But, what better way to get an army than to free an army and invite them to help liberate the rest of the human race," Aurik replied.

"You aren't thinking about trying to free them, are you? That place is a fortress!"

"I wasn't until you mentioned it."

"Whoa! Wait a minute!" Jordon waved his hands up in front of him. "I never suggested that you go on a suicide mission!"

Aurik smiled.

"Maybe not, but you gave me the idea."

"You can't be serious!"

"As ever."

"You guys are crazy. You are all going to get yourselves killed."

"Maybe, but at least we will die for a cause, and die free," Aurik replied. "I'm going to get heading back. Stay safe, Jordon, and thanks for your help." Aurik lifted the grain sacks.

Jordon nodded as Aurik turned to leave. "Well, good luck," he said as he too turned to head back to his home.

***

When Aurik returned to the cavern, he found Jessica staring at the communications console screen, the glow lighting up her ebony face with an almost angelic glow.

He dropped the supply sacks at the entrance and quietly sauntered over to her, not wanting to make too much noise, as the rest of his team were fast asleep.

"Keeping watch, are you?" Aurik asked.

Jessica looked up, tapping the next console over.

"I saw you coming a dozen yards out," she replied. "Take a look at this, Aurik," she requested as she closed the readout on the screen, she was reading and scrolled through a list of files. "We really hit the jackpot here. All of these files are inventory lists, shift schedules, equipment specs, all by department." She tapped an icon on the inventory list, and another window popped up. "These are all supply request and shipment schedules into and out of the compound. It's everything we need to know to get an upper hand on the N'Roth." She again closed the window and tapped another couple of icons, pulling up two more pop-up windows. "These we have to get. One is some kind of healing device that heals major wounds – say like a broken leg – in a matter of minutes. The other is a communications array. With that we will be able to listen in on any communications going through their coms."

"Those would be helpful," Aurik replied. "We can finally get Kyle back on his feet with that healing device."

"That, and if something like that happens again, we can heal the injured parties and get them back into the field in a matter of minutes," Jessica added.

"Okay. Let's discuss this more tomorrow. Who has last watch tonight?"

"You do. It was supposed to be Yin, but I switched you two so you could get some rest before watch, so she is taking watch next shift instead of you."

"I see. I appreciate that. We have a lot to discuss tomorrow." Aurik patted her on the shoulder. "Keep up with the good work on finding useful supplies. Make a list of everything you find that we might be able to acquire."

Jessica nodded, and Aurik turned in for the night.

***

Aurik began cooking breakfast after his watch was over, knowing the smell of freshly cooked food would arouse the others. Jordon was able to supply them with several weeks of rations as well as a few days of fresh fruit, vegetables, corn, and bread for them, so they enjoyed a freshly cooked meal.

One by one, Aurik's counterparts awoke, and when the meal was ready, they relished in the variety of fresh food.

"We really need to start gathering from this forest," Kyle commented through a mouth full of food.

"Well, when you are better, we'll make that your responsibility," Yin replied.

"Gladly!" Kyle said.

"There is a possibility that we can acquire an N'Roth healing device that will heal your leg," Jessica mentioned.

"Really?" Kyle asked, stuffing his mouth with another slice of an oddly shaped purple fruit.

"Yes," Aurik answered. "The link up to the N'Roth computer proved more fruitful than we could have imagined. Jessica compiled a list of items the N'Roth have that would prove extremely useful in our fight." Aurik paused, gauging the reactions of his friends. "It's dangerous and risky, but if we pull it off, we can come out of this with a real advantage here."

"You're suggesting we pull a heist on the N'Roth compound, right?" Sarah asked.

Aurik nodded.

"Do you really think we can do it?" she asked.

"I think we have to try," Aurik replied.

"Jordon told me that...," He looked at Jessica, "the second signal you found…" He turned back to the rest of the group. "is a labor camp."

"A labor camp?" Yin replied in shock.

"Yes, and I want us to free it."

"Free the labor camp? Have you even seen it?" Jessica added.

"No, I don't really even know where it is, but think about it. If we succeed in freeing the camp, we will have literally gained an army overnight."

The team glanced back and forth at each other in silence a few moments.

"Well, I say let's do it," Kyle said, who had stopped stuffing food into his mouth at this point. "Especially if it means that y'all get that dang healing thing to fix my leg!"

Aurik nodded.

"Okay, let's do it," Jessica added, and Yin and Sarah both nodded in agreement.

"Okay!" Aurik said. "Now, we need to make a plan. Jessica, when we are done with breakfast, you see if you can find blueprints or schematics or something of the N'Roth compound."

Jessica nodded.

"We'll also need to see if we can find out exactly where everything is being stored, and let's see if we can find the weapons lockers."

Aurik turned to Sarah.

"While we're at it, Sarah, see if you can come up with something to cause some damage in that facility and maybe see if you can rig up some small explosives or something as a distraction."

Sarah nodded.

They finished their meals quickly after that, then began preparations for the incursion into the enemy compound. Jessica and Sarah worked on their assignments while Aurik, Kyle, and Yin created a plan of attack. After that, Aurik and Yin gathered anticipated items needed for the mission.

17

The four waited until well into the night to begin their mission, choosing the wall in the alley of the market section of the town as the infiltration point into the compound. They carried minimal equipment; each only carrying an N'Roth rifle, a large pack that Jordon had procured for them, and Yin and Aurik carried a ladder he had made from the branches of the trees near their base so they could scale the wall quickly and easily.

He stood now near the top rung of the ladder, peering into the compound vehicle lot. It was dark, with only a few lights in the open lot, leaving a lot of shadows for potential cover.

The lot had half a dozen vehicle types. Aurik noticed that none of them had wheels. He saw a gate at the far entrance that looked more like the doorways of the ship that they had escaped only days before. He took note of the nearest accessible exit, just in case the mission went sideways.

He scanned the rest of the vehicle lot, noting no N'Roth patrols, and when he was satisfied that it was clear, he quickly slid over the edge, dropping silently to the ground.

Yin, Jessica, and Sarah followed close behind, each landing silently to the ground as well.

"Looks like they don't have any security," Sarah commented.

"That's probably because there has never been any real need for security here before," Aurik replied.

"Well, let's hope that the lack of security is consistent throughout the compound," Yin added.

"When I checked the roster, there was only a skeleton crew scheduled for this time at night," Jessica reported.

"Good. Hopefully, that will make it easier," Aurik said. "Let's go."

Aurik led his team through the shadows to the entrance inside the N'Roth compound, then turned around.

"Everybody ready?" he asked. The team nodded a collective affirmative. "Okay, here we go." Aurik pressed the panel to open the entryway, and the door hissed open.

The squad immediately rushed in. Aurik and Jessica darted off into a corridor to the right while Yin and Sarah sprinted straight down the main corridor.

Thanks to Jordon's supply run, each member of the team had a tablet that Jessica had uploaded pre-determined routes onto from the console's schematics.

Sarah and Yin were to head to the weapon's locker and general storage compartment. Jessica and Aurik were to acquire the antennae array in another section of storage compartments that housed N'Roth computer supplies and parts, and the healing device from the infirmary.

If it all went as planned, they would be in and out in minutes unnoticed. If they needed to, they had placed crude explosives around the market as a distraction. They hoped none of them would be necessary.

***

Aurik and Jessica reached the first of their destinations and hastily ducked inside before the door had even finished hissing open.

They scanned the room for any N'Roth, finding none, and immediately went about searching out the antennae array and whatever else Jessica deemed worthy.

The storage compartment was meticulously organized with shelves stacked to the brim. There was a table near the entrance with several tablets on it, and Jessica snatched one up. The tablet blinked on as she picked it up, and she scanned it.

"Perfect," she said as she handed it to Aurik, and grabbed a second one which blinked on as well. "This will make it easier to find what we are looking for." She tapped in a search for the communications array, and the tablet blipped into a map of the storage compartment with a highlighted path to the designated coordinates.

"Yes!" She held out the tablet to Aurik. "Here, switch." Aurik obeyed. "You get the array, and I'll look around for whatever else will come in handy for us." Aurik nodded, and

Jessica went to tapping away on the tablet as Aurik followed the map.

***

Sarah and Yin raced down the corridor to the stairwell indicated on their route. Yin reached it first and slid to a halt, causing Sarah to slam into her as she happened to choose that moment to glance behind them to check the rear.

Yin held back a cry as Sarah knocked her off balance. She recovered quickly, but not before she stumbled into the open entryway to the stairwell.

It just so happened that precisely what she was trying to avoid by stopping before the stairwell came to pass. An N'Roth soldier was climbing down the stairs as she stumbled into the open.

She let out a curse and jumped into action. She darted for the stairway rail, punched off of it onto the opposite wall, and pushed off of the wall into a spin kick, striking the soldier square in the side of the face before it could even bring its radio up. The soldier let out a scream as Yin's foot slammed so hard into its face that it slammed into the wall with a loud crack, the wall prematurely silencing its shriek as he slumped to the floor.

Sarah jumped around the corner to see the N'Roth falling to the floor and its radio tumbling down the stairway with thud after thud until it landed at her feet. She snatched it up and shoved it into her pack.

Yin quickly peered up the staircase, then grabbed the N'Roth's arm.

"Come on," she ordered. Sarah understood and grabbed its other arm. They hefted the soldier up, pulling its arms over their shoulders and dragged it up the flight of stairs.

When they reached the next level, Yin peered down the corridor.

"Clear," she said, and the two women pulled the alien down the corridor and into the armory, dropping it to the side of the sliding door.

As soon as the door hissed shut, the two began snatching items and dropping them into their packs.

The weapon's compartment had racks along each wall except the entry wall and a center row of racks facing both ways. Along one wall, the shelves contained rifles, and the opposite wall held rows of pistols. The two stands that were placed in the center of the room held small items such as radios, life sign detectors, chargers, and batteries of some kind, knives, and weapon belt straps. Along the far back wall sat racks that contained oddly shaped canisters and containers, along with small spherical devices.

The far wall was the last to be raided as Sarah and Yin examined each item type, trying to figure out what they were. Sarah figured out pretty quickly that they were some sort of explosive devices, although, with some of them, she had no idea what they were. Many resembled earth-style explosives that they still used in their time, before they went into stasis.

They filled their packs up only halfway with items, skipping the rifles all together as they were large, tossing even the unfamiliar explosive devices in their packs, then left for their second objective.

***

Aurik found the array quickly. It was in a bulky black case, and when he opened it to make sure it was the correct item, he quickly realized he wouldn't be able to tell if it was the wrong item anyway. As far as he could tell, it looked like an array: a bulky centerpiece with the N'Roth wire conduits and several antennae reeds, all secured in a foam-like material. He shut the container, seeing a handle, he didn't bother with stuffing it in his pack. He doubted it would even fit, but hefted it out of its storage slot. He immediately noticed it was lighter than it looked, which he was grateful for.

He found Jessica stuffing her pack full of various electrical supplies and equipment, to include some much-needed wiring casing and toolsets.

Soon they were out the door of the armory and headed to the infirmary. It was only two corridors down, so they didn't have a problem getting there, but the moment the door to the infirmary opened, they leapt into action.

Jessica had taken note that there were always three N'Roth stationed in the infirmary at all times and so it didn't come as a surprise that three N'Roth were roaming about the infirmary.

They dispatched two soldiers swiftly as they were in the first room, preoccupied with their duties, but the third was near the back and heard the rifle blasts. It raced for the intercom, dodging blast after blast from both Jessica and Aurik as it fled across the room.

The blasts scorched the walls and consoles as the two frantically fired on the N'Roth, and it desperately dodged the onslaught of rifle blasts until it finally reached the intercom. With nowhere else for it to go, Jessica and Aurik both fired several shots into the alien as it tried to speak into the intercom.

The enemy soldier fell silent mid-word as the blasts jolted it to the ground in a dead, smoldering heap.

The air filled with the foul stench of scorched flesh and the onslaught of rifle fire brought a thin cloud of smoke wafting throughout the room.

A scratchy N'Roth voice burst through the intercom, requesting the dead N'Roth repeat the message.

"We'd better hurry," Aurik said. "They'll undoubtedly be sending someone to check on him."

Jessica nodded and scanned the room for the healing device, finding it mere seconds later.

"Here!" she exclaimed, rushing over to it.

It was surprisingly compact. Aurik noticed that the edges used to surround the body parts to be healed folded and slid in and out to make the device fit larger appendages. In full size, it would fit around a broad torso.

Aurik fiddled with it, compacting it so he could fit it into his pack while Jessica hastily snatched anything loose and small enough to fit in her pack.

"I've got it!" Aurik said. Without hesitation, Jessica rushed for the door.

***

Yin and Sarah reached their second objective without resistance and, once inside, started searching for their list of items. It was a small storage room, and so it was easy to find most of what they were looking for.

They found the first aid, food rations, and power supplies almost immediately. The tablets and tool kits were farther toward the back of the storage room, but they found them fairly quickly as well. They cleared the facility out of each and began tossing whatever they saw in their packs until each bag was so full that they could barely close them. Noticing in the process what looked like tiny portable power supplies and digital storage sticks, they emptied those contents into their packs as well and headed back for their rendezvous point.

***

Aurik and Jessica rushed out of the infirmary door, Aurik squeezing through first with the bulky antennae array case and raced down the corridor, Jessica on his heels.

Aurik stopped in his tracks as he rounded the corner, coming face-to-face with an N'Roth soldier with its two counterparts behind it. Jessica barely had time to stop herself, before slamming into Aurik.

The N'Roth brought up its rifle. Aurik didn't have his own rifle at the ready and Jessica, behind him was far too close and didn't have a clear shot, so he flung the array case up, knocking the rifle away as the N'Roth fired harmlessly into the corridor wall, then slammed headfirst into the soldier.

Aurik and the N'Roth went stumbling into the two soldiers, which allowed Jessica the time to bring her weapon up and fire a round into the chest of one of the two soldiers but not before the other fired a shot at Jessica.

Jessica dove to the ground, barely dodging the lethal energy blast, attempting a roll when she hit the ground, however, the added weight and bulkiness of her pack prevented her from rolling. She not only couldn't roll, but she also had lodged her rifle under her, expecting to be able to free it and bring it around for a shot. Now without the ability to roll and her weapon stuck, she was an easy target. She scrambled to pull her rifle out and maneuver to a better combat position.

Aurik pulled away from the N'Roth soldier, still holding tightly to the array case. He didn't anticipate the quick reaction of the N'Roth and noticed too late the soldier's muzzle rising. He brought his own up, then his world went black.

18

Sarah and Yin quickly made their way through the corridor, down the stairwell, and back outside into the vehicle lot. They were surprised, however, that Aurik and Jessica were not back from their own mission yet. They still wasted no time, though, and the two women found the smallest vehicle with a covered bed and tossed their heavy packs inside.

Yin jumped into the bed while Sarah hopped up into the cab, scanning the dashboard.

The readouts were in N'Roth, but thankfully she could read it well enough. She quickly found the ignition button and direction controls. It was much like the shuttle they had stolen the day that they had awakened from stasis. Like almost everything, it was digitalized. The dashboard had lit up as she opened the door and jumped in, making it that much easier to steal.

"Come on, Aurik, Jessica. Hurry up," she said as she tapped on the dashboard's console.

After a few more seconds, Sarah hopped back out of the cab, and made her way to the back of the bed of the truck. "I'm getting worried. They should've beaten us back here."

"I know," Yin replied as she scooted closer to her friend.

"We'll give them two more minutes, then I'm going after them," Sarah said.

Yin nodded.

***

Jessica scrambled as fast as she could to maneuver her rifle under her. She knew that she didn't have enough time to bring it up and around before her enemy shot her. He had the advantage in every way; mobility, speed, an open target. She, on the other hand, had limited mobility as she was prone on the floor. She was severely handicapped in her speed because of the fifty-pound pack weighing her down. She could barely even see her target. She was in a bad situation.

She could see her foe's feet as it took a step closer. She knew the N'Roth was about to fire. She had to think fast. Think creatively.

As fast as she could, she slid the barrel of her alien rifle toward her foe and fired.

The rifle blast hit its target, scorching her enemy's foot, and bringing with it the smell of burning rubber and flesh.

The N'Roth screamed as the pain exploded through its foot, and the force from the energy bolt knocked it off balance. The creature let out another howl of pain as it slammed its good knee into the hard floor with a smack.

Jessica didn't hesitate. She twisted her hip just enough to lift her rifle a couple of inches, then fired again, and again, and again and again, each blast hitting its mark. The N'Roth jerked with every bolt that hit it, leaving a searing scorch mark that melted the creature's uniform to its flesh. Fresh puffs of smoke rising with every blast that connected with her target, along with the foul stench of burning alien flesh. Then, the alien soldier collapsed right on top of her pack, dead.

She let out a half scream – half sigh as the added weight from the soldier with her pack pinned her even tighter to the ground.

***

Aurik's head pounded, and his chest ached. He felt like he had been hit by a falling anvil. He shook his head to clear his mind and immediately regretted it as the pounding erupted like a volcano, and he groaned, closing his eyes in a futile effort to ease the pain.

Realization flooded through him, and he jumped to his feet. He dropped to his knees once again as a new wave of dizziness shot over him.

He saw Jessica, then, inching her way out from under a dead N'Roth.

"Jessica," he moaned, struggling for words as the dizziness and pain in his head threatened to overwhelm him.

"Aurik!" she exclaimed as she finally wiggled her way free and crawled to his side. "What happened?"

"I don't know," Aurik replied, barely able to get the words out.

She noticed the blood on the floor next to him, and her eyes went wide as she touched the back of his head. Aurik winced at the touch, and she felt the warmth of his blood.

"Oh God. We've got to get you out of here. Can you walk?"

Aurik didn't answer, he grabbed her shoulder and pushed himself up.

She caught him as he began to fall and stood to her feet as well.

"There's no way you can walk," she said as she set him back down to the floor. "Hold on." She unstrapped her pack, set it down, then unstrapped Aurik's. He fell forward at the sudden loss of weight and caught himself, just as he passed out, slowing his descent so he didn't smack hard onto the floor, but gently dropped prone.

"Aurik! Hold on!" Jessica exclaimed as she strapped the two packs together, then rolled him on top of them.

She snatched up the array case, ignoring the scorch mark on it, and kicked aside Aurik's rifle, then began dragging him down the corridor.

She heard the N'Roth radio chirp on, and a voice ask for a report.

She pulled harder.

***

Sarah banged on the N'Roth transport. "That's it. I'm going after them!" Yin nodded and jumped down from the back of the truck.

"Me too."

The two raced to the entrance into the compound, and into the corridor, weapons up and ready. They turned down the corridor to the right and saw Jessica dragging Aurik.

The two rushed to her side, Sarah slinging her weapon to help pull Aurik while Yin kept her rifle up, keeping watch on both ends of the corridor.

240

Suddenly, an alarm sounded, and seconds later, another squad of N'Roth rounded the corner Jessica and Aurik had turned only moments before.

Yin fired an onslaught of energy bolts, hitting one unfortunate soldier before any of them could open fire. They retreated back around the corner.

Yin did not ease up on her attack. She continued to fire blast after blast down the corridor. She knew she wouldn't hit any of the soldiers that took cover, but all she needed to do was keep them from firing back. She hoped that as long as she kept firing, none of them would dare try and chance getting hit by returning fire.

Seconds later, the four stopped at the corner of the corridor, and Sarah peeked down the main hallway.

"Clear!" she yelled, and the four advanced through the exit into the vehicle lot.

***

Yin was the last out, still laying down cover fire. By the time she reached the doorway, a thick haze of smoke hovered at the end of the corridor she had been firing down, and the wall had more black scorch marks than the original white before she had started firing.

She was just about to turn tail and run when her rifle overheated or ran out of power, she didn't know which. It just stopped firing. The instant her weapon stopped, she found herself facing an onslaught of energy blasts herself. She dove through the doorway as a dozen deadly bolts passed inches from her.

She rolled to her feet without skipping a beat in her step, and sprinted back toward the door, pressing her back up against the wall just next to the entryway.

Before the door finished hissing shut, it whooshed back open, and the three N'Roth soldiers left untouched by her weapon's fire raced through the entryway, their muzzles up.

The second the aliens passed the threshold Yin burst into a flurry of activity.

***

Jessica and Sarah pulled Aurik through the threshold out into the vehicle lot, and Sarah directed Jessica to their getaway truck. They both saw Yin narrowly dodge the energy bolts.

"Go help Yin," Jessica ordered. Sarah didn't even bother to acknowledge Jessica, she unslung her rifle and took cover behind a nearby vehicle.

19

Yin leapt from the wall into a high side kick, bringing her foot up into the cheek of the first alien that passed by her. It let out a shriek, stumbling into the soldier next to it as Yin planted her foot, using the momentum from her side kick to propel her into a modified spin kick. She jumped forward as she brought her back leg up, stretching her knee up and out, so it collided with the last N'Roth's face with a sharp crack. The soldier smacked hard into the entryway door frame with another crack as Yin landed.

Again, Yin continued using her momentum, pivoting on her heel into a spin as she flung her rifle at the soldier she had struck in the cheek, and then placed a hand to the ground, turning her spin into an altered butterfly kick. Using her fixed hand for additional balance, Yin twisted her hips, spreading her feet out wide and kicking them up high, slamming the ball of one foot after the other into her opponent's face, finally sending the worn-down soldier to the ground unconscious.

Yin pushed off the ground as she landed her feet, pushing herself back up into a standing position and was just about to begin a spin kick into her last opponent when an energy bolt sent it to the ground with a scorch mark on its side. Yin looked up to see Sarah stand up from the cover of an N'Roth transport, and they shared an appreciative nod.

Yin rushed for the getaway vehicle.

Sarah, being closer, got there first and finished helping Jessica lift Aurik and the packs into the truck.

Yin hopped in and helped drag Aurik to the front of the bed, and Sarah darted around to the driver's seat, powering it up while Jessica hopped in the back as well.

"Hold on!" Sarah yelled through the cab wall, jerking the truck into action.

Yin and Jessica didn't even have time to grab for the benches along the sides of the truck bed before Sarah punched the anti-gravity propelled truck forward, and they both fell to the bed floor. Seconds later, the vehicle plowed through the vehicle lot gate with a loud bang, and everyone inside was jolted around.

The two saw the entryway doors swinging back into place as they sped off down the path, and were relieved when they saw that no N'Roth followed.

They wasted no time making their way back to their cave, following the road back around town toward Benjamin's farm. Once they neared the farm, Sarah pulled off of the road, and the three struggled to unload Aurik and the packs from the back of the truck.

"We need to heal Aurik, quickly!" Sarah said as she looked over his head wound and checked his eyes. "This is as good a time as any to see if that healing device works."

Jessica nodded and wrestled the healing device out of the pack.

"We have to get that vehicle out of the road, and move Aurik a little into the cover of the forest," Sarah added. "I will stay with Aurik and heal him with the device. You two go drive that truck off of that cliff a few miles away."

"Okay," Jessica replied, handing Sarah the bulky piece of technology, then grabbed one of the packs and rushed into the brush.

Yin followed suit, both returning and snatching up the last two packs while Sarah moved Aurik just a few feet into the cover of the trees, the healing device resting on his chest.

"We'll meet you back here as soon as we stash that truck," Jessica said.

"Try and be back before dawn," Sarah said.

Jessica and Yin both nodded in understanding and hopped into the cab of the anti-grav truck, speeding off down the road and disappearing into the forest back the way they had just come from.

***

Sarah pulled out the extending arms of the healing device to fit around Aurik's head, and as gently as she could, slid the device under his head.

She found the power button quickly enough and began the healing process. From what she gathered when reading over the specs for the healing unit was that the device itself scanned whatever was set within its sensory appendages and immediately began healing the broken bone.

She heard a slight, low pitched hum as the machine lit up, then panels on the underside of its expandable appendages began glowing a blue pulsating light. She waited, acutely aware of its humming, and hoped it couldn't be heard from more than a few feet away.

Sarah filled the long minutes waiting for Aurik to heal by stacking the four packs next to a tree and quickly made her way back to the road to see if any N'Roth had by chance followed them. It was still a calm, quiet night, at least around Benjamin's farm.

***

Yin and Jessica finally reached the cliff and set the controls to the antigravity vehicle to cruise and watched it plummet into the dried-up riverbed to best demolish the heavy tank-like transport, then the two women started back towards

Benjamin's farm in a slow jog.

***

When Yin and Jessica finally reached Sarah and Aurik,

Aurik was awake and leaning against a tree, his hand resting

over his eyes.

"It worked!" Jessica said as she saw Aurik.

"It sure did," Aurik replied in a quiet tone. "But I'm not

sure if I wouldn't have preferred death. My head is pounding."

He slowly stood, resting a palm on the tree. "Enough

complaining, it'll be light soon, and I'm going to slow us

down. I can tell you that for sure. Every movement makes my

head throb."

"We'll take it slow," Sarah said. "We'll keep you in the

middle, I'll take point, and Yin will take up the rear. That way,

if we run into any trouble, you can just take cover."

"Agreed, I don't think I would be much help in any

kind of combat right now."

The four took up their positions, sliding their packs on, Jessica helping Aurik with his so he wouldn't need to bend over or move too much, and the weary team began their journey back to the cave.

***

Well after the break of dawn, the team finally made it back to their hidden base. Aurik dropped his pack at the entryway and went straight to his sleeping gear without a word.

Although Sarah was still concerned that he might have a concussion, she didn't stop him from resting.

The rest of them dropped their packs along with Aurik's. Jessica immediately went about inspecting the array and integrating it into their console system, while Sarah focused on preparing the healing device for Kyle's leg, and Yin began unpacking the packs.

"We need to make some shelves," Yin demanded as she looked around for somewhere to place their newly acquired supplies. She decided to use her own sleeping gear as a mat to make sure the items stayed clean and dry.

By the time Yin was finished setting all of their new equipment on her sleeping gear, Kyle's leg had been fully healed. He hesitantly stood to his feet, not entirely trusting the N'Roth tool, but as he stood, he noticed there was no pain, only a little soreness.

"Hot Dog!" Kyle yelled excitedly as he bounced a couple of times on his freshly healed leg. "That darn thing really does work!"

"Now you can start foraging for food," Yin replied at his excitement. He stopped bouncing and turned toward her.

"As I said before, if it meant I could walk again, then that is a small price to pay."

"You act like you were never going to walk again. It was only a broken leg," Yin said.

"Ha! Well, you try being stuck in bed while everyone else gets to have fun!"

Yin smiled.

"So, did ya'll get any cool weapons?" he asked.

"No, just a few rifles and those handguns. We couldn't find any other gun types in that armory." Yin replied.

"Well, shucks. I'll just have to tinker with those things and see if I can add a few bells and whistles, then." Kyle bent low to inspect the new supply of weapons.

Yin moved to stand next to Jessica. "How's it going with the array?"

"Well, it looks like it's still in good shape, despite being shot with an energy bolt." Jessica pointed to the case on the floor next to them. "But we won't know for sure until we get it integrated into the system."

"Okay. What do you need us to do?"

"We'll eventually need to put the array somewhere high, and this being a cave, we will need to use a bunch of that N'Roth wire to connect to it because the rock will block the signal otherwise."

"Gotcha."

"I'm going to see if I can set up a relay from the array itself wirelessly, and just set the relay right outside the cave entrance so we use less of that N'Roth wiring."

"Okay. We'll scout around the cave for a high point to place the array."

"We'll need to camouflage it too," Jessica added.

Yin nodded.

"Kyle, want to make yourself useful, finally?" Yin jested.

Kyle gave her a quick, playful scowl, then hopped up from inspecting the various weapons on Yin's bedroll.

"I suppose I need to start pulling my weight around here again," he replied as he strode over to Jessica and Yin.

"That's a lot of weight." Yin quipped.

Again, Kyle gave a playful scowl.

"We need to find a high place to put that." Yin pointed to the array. "Then we need to camouflage it."

"My first mission since being back on my feet!" Kyle smiled. "I'll go take a look around." With that, Kyle happily left the confines of the cave that he had been stuck in for days

and began his search for a spot to place the array.

20

Kyle followed the edge of the large hill that housed their secret cave base and found a small ledge just a few feet from the entrance.

The dense brush opened up into a clearing that left the side of the small mountain open to the sky, and the ledge stood just a few dozen feet above head height.

Kyle scrutinized the mountainside after he spotted the ledge, noticing how jagged and uneven it was. It wasn't a sheer cliff, but a very, very steep sloping rock face.

"Well, what better way to see if my leg is fully healed," he murmured to himself. "Probably a bad idea. I'll probably break my leg again." Kyle studied the first few feet of the rock face carefully, noting all of the tiny jutting pieces and small indentations of the cliffside for hand and footholds, then began his ascent.

He climbed up the dangerously steep mountainside cautiously, checking and double-checking his foot and handholds before pulling himself up to the next. He went slowly, and tired quickly, and when he finally reached the ledge, he was out of breath and gasping for air. He saw that it was much deeper than he had thought and, to his surprise, noticed a small cave entrance.

"Aw heck, that figures," he said out of breath and pulled himself onto the ledge.

He rolled onto his back, breathing heavily and staring out into the morning sky.

He rested a couple of minutes, enjoying the view. He hadn't taken one minute to enjoy his surroundings since crashing on the planet, so being cooped up inside that cave, even just for a couple of days, made him appreciate the open sky.

After a few minutes, he climbed back onto his feet and peered into the entrance to the cave. He couldn't see more than a few feet into the mouth of the entrance, but he saw something that piqued his interest, but he couldn't decide if it was just his

imagination or if there was actually something in the cave. He

saw a tiny, almost imperceptible glow.

He took just a couple tentative steps into the mouth of

the cave, then waited for his eyes to adjust to the low light.

Still, he couldn't make out what the glow was, but he was sure

now that he wasn't imagining it.

Something *was* glowing inside the cave.

Kyle set a hand on the cave wall to use as a guide as he

took a few more steps closer to the glowing object, and felt the

wetness of the rock. It was a warm wetness, not the cold, damp,

condensation one would expect from a cave, but warm. He

noticed then, as well, as he stepped further into the cave

entrance, that it was warmer in this tunnel than any of the

others he had ventured through. It didn't feel airy and cold, but

warm and humid, somehow.

He slid his hand along the rock as he inched his way

further into the cave. He went slowly, keeping his eyes down at

his feet, not wanting to step into a hole or a crack in the

darkness. It grew increasingly more difficult for him to see his feet, and he eventually slowed even more as he started shuffling on the ground with his feet to avoid any dips, slants, or holes.

He had only gone a few dozen feet more when he noticed a brighter glowing from deeper into the cave. He was close enough now to make out what it was that had initially caught his eye. It was a single leaf. A small green glowing leaf.

He inched his way to the leaf and plucked it from the rock, and held it up close. It was a quarter the size of his palm, puffy, thick, short, and wide. He rubbed the leaf in his palm with his thumb. It was soft and fuzzy.

He looked up towards the glowing farther down the tunnel.

"Stupid idea, probably," he whispered to himself. "I can't see a thing," he murmured, and continued further into the dark cave, the leaf still in his hand.

As he neared the glowing, he began hearing more and more skittering bugs, and felt warm cave condensation dripping on him in increasing intervals. Again, he reached the glowing light, and this time it was a small cluster of leaves. He noticed as well that several insects were feeding on the leaves. As he peered down the tunnel, he saw even more. Their glow was much more visible, so he knew it was an even larger cluster than the one he stood by.

He inched his way further into the dark cave, noticing more and more bugs, more and more condensation, and more and more glow from the luminescent plants.

As he neared the next cluster, he noticed that he could just barely see his feet. The glow from the plants were giving off more and more light for him to see!

He continued deeper and soon could see well enough to walk casually as the cavern walls were covered every few feet with large patches of the glowing leaves.

Then he rounded a sharp corner, and he gasped in astonishment. The tunnel opened up into a massive cavern filled almost entirely with the luminescent plant life. Bugs and lizards scurried away from him as he stepped further into the warm chamber. Awed at the sight, Kyle ambled around the chamber, seeing that the center was so overgrown with the leaves that it looked almost like a forest. As the glowing leaves spread out from that, they slowly diminished until there were sporadic patches of leaves growing between rocks and in cracks.

He saw, as well, a moss of some sort that clung to the rocks and protruded from the cracks. Though the moss was less frequent, it was easily distinguishable from the leaves. The moss was several shades darker than the leaves and added a pleasant accent color to the bright green of the main plant.

The moss and leaves climbed up onto the walls and hung like chandeliers from the ceiling. It was a marvelous sight.

Kyle neared the center, where the highest concentration of plant life was located, and saw that there was a massive fissure that the plants grew from, and he knew that there must be some sort of geological heat source emanating from it.

He eventually took in all he could and began investigating the other cave tunnels that he noticed when he was observing the newly found cavern.

He walked a few feet into each, noticing the plant life dwindling significantly after several dozen yards. When he couldn't see, he doubled back from each new tunnel he explored.

He found each appeared to go on beyond the growths of the plant, and he decided to gather a large handful of the leaves to light his way through the blackness of the tunnels.

A few minutes later, he began back down the tunnel that he figured led in the direction of the main cavern. He hoped that there would be an opening into one of the main passageways that he had charted already.

He started to get discouraged as he ventured through this new tunnel with his makeshift glow-stick when he noticed that it felt like the path was angling up rather than down. He knew he was above the main entrance, and if he was going further up, then chances were he wouldn't be heading in the right direction.

Then the tunnel suddenly split. One direction angled up, and the other path angled down. Both angled dangerously steep.

Kyle chose the downward angle, even though he knew that he would regret going further if he hit a dead end and had to climb back up.

The tunnel grew smaller and smaller as he half-climbed, half-slid down the path. After just a few minutes, he saw the faint glow of light ahead. Not the glow of the luminescence from the plant life, but the bright white light from another, artificial, light source.

He moved faster, knowing the light to be from the main chamber or somewhere close to it because he could now hear the faint voices of his counterparts.

The closer he got to the chamber, the smaller the tunnel became, until he had to crawl flat on his stomach, then suddenly, the tunnel opened up into the main chamber.

It wasn't what Kyle had expected, though. He had been crawling so fast down the ever-steepening tunnel that by the time he reached the opening, he was more falling than crawling, and when the tunnel opened up into the main chamber, he tumbled out, landing on the hard cave floor with a resounding crack.

He let out a scream as his freshly healed leg crumbled under him with a sickening crack, and a surge of excruciating pain rattled through his body.

21

Kyle woke to the humming of the healing device around his leg.

"He's awake!" Yin shouted across the chamber, then leaned over. "Are you alright? Is anything else broken other than your leg?" she asked.

"Nah. Nothing too bad. Just sore all around, that's all.

"Where did you come from? How did you get up there?"

"Well, I found another tunnel when I was lookin for a place to put that array. I found a spot, by the way, and I found something crazy. Some kind of glowing plant life," Kyle said.

"Bio-luminescent plant life," Jessica replied. "That's fantastic. I'll have to take a look at it."

"Well, I'll show you when my leg heals up again," Kyle said.

"That will have to wait," Aurik said as he strolled in from the joining chamber. "First, we're going to scout that labor camp."

"Aurik. How are you feeling?" Sarah asked.

"Still got the headache, but it's not quite as bad," he replied. "We all need to get some sleep. Kyle, you're on first watch. As soon as your leg is healed, everybody is going to get some rest. At nightfall, we're all going to check out that labor camp. Kyle, after about four hours, wake me up for next watch."

"Kyle should be all healed up in just a minute," Sarah reported. "When these lights go off, and the humming stops, it's done healing him. It's pretty easy to take off. Kyle can do it himself."

"Okay then, Kyle, take that off when you are done. The rest of you get some shut-eye." Aurik ordered.

They all nodded and headed for their bedrolls, Sarah explaining how to remove the device from Kyle's leg before leaving Kyle to his watch.

Aurik woke the squad one by one, offering them a bowl of chili that Jordan had provided with the last supply run. After they had each had their fill, the squad made their way to the labor camp.

Less than an hour later, they heard the camp before they saw it. They heard the rumbling of conveyor belts and the crunching of rocks. Then, when the forest cleared and fell off into a ditch a few feet after the clearing, they saw it.

The labor camp was in the center of a large ditch that was several dozen feet deep. Surrounding the ditch, lights faced inward, and along the far side were rows of conveyor belts that carried rocks up and out of the ditch, dropping them into large basins set near the edge of the ditch.

Throughout the compound were clusters of workers with pickaxes breaking apart massive rocks into pieces, or carting rocks to the conveyor belts and transferring the rocks onto the belts while other workers stood at the edges of the ditch picking at the rocks along the edge.

Several dozen N'Roth soldiers patrolled both the inside perimeter as well as the rest of the camp as well as along the erected lights.

A tower stood on each of the two conjoining cliff sides to the edge that housed the conveyor belts, both several stories above the edge of the ditch with several enclosed levels.

A line of, what looked like to the squad, troop tents spanned across the center of the quarry.

A whistle sounded, and the workers began plodding to a large table that stood near the tents.

The squad watched as the workers dropped their tools in a pile next to the table and stood in line.

"What are they doing?" Sarah asked.

"Looks like they are finished for the day," Kyle replied.

"Look." Jessica nodded to a second line in which the leading worker held out a wrist, and an N'Roth swiped a device over the worker's arm. The worker shuffled down the table taking something and entered one of the tents while the process was repeated with the next prisoner, and the next, and the next.

"Looks like they are being scanned," Kyle said.

"Benjamin did tell us that tracking chips are inserted into people," Yin added. "They must be using them to keep some kind of records or something."

"Okay, let's circle around and take note of anything we can use to our advantage. Kyle, Jessica, Yin, you three go that way." Aurik pointed to his right. "Sarah and I will go this way." He pointed to the left. "We will meet behind the center conveyer belt. Let's go."

Without acknowledgment, the three disappeared into the shadows to the right as Aurik, and Sarah vanished into the darkness to the left.

***

The groups met up at the designated rendezvous point and briefly discussed their routes, making sure to include any details that they could use to their advantage.

"Okay," Aurik said. "Let's head back to the cave. We'll start an assault plan when we get back and prepare all day tomorrow. Tomorrow night, we free these workers.

"When we get back, Yin and Kyle, you two gather anticipated supplies. Sarah and Jessica, you two figure out how we might be able to disable those arm trackers. I'll work on an assault plan based on our observations here." The squad nodded, and the five made their way back to the cave.

***

The five didn't hesitate to begin their assigned tasks with Aurik isolating himself in a corner and forming his attack strategy. He occasionally visited with his counterparts who were diligently working, getting updates on their progress, giving suggestions, and double-checking intel. Near sunset, he called the squad over to him.

"Okay, I made a schematic of the prison camp," he said as he knelt down in front of a makeshift model of the ditch made from various items he found throughout the cave.

"Gather around," he ordered. The four surrounded the model and took a knee.

Aurik pointed to a row of rocks. "Okay, this is the row of conveyor belts. The two cans on either side are those towers." Aurik pointed to three utensils beside one of the cans. "Those are the three transports that Kyle said were near the tower." He pointed to another smaller can on the opposite side of the model. "Here is the generator for the lights that Sarah and I saw." Pointing to a line of utensils near the generator, he added, "This is the road in and out of the ditch. Everybody get that?"

The squad nodded.

"Good. We are doing this in three phases. Phase one, take out all the perimeter guards quietly. No shots fired. We'll break up into three teams. Jessica and Kyle, me and Sarah, and Yin. Yin, with your combat skills, I think you can handle taking out guards swiftly and quietly by yourself, am I right?"

Yin nodded.

"We'll spread out. Yin will start from the farthest belt, here." He pointed to the last *conveyer belt* rock. Aurik pointed to the opposite side of the perimeter. "Sarah, and I will make our way from where we first discovered the site, here, and make our way to Yin. Kyle, you and Jessica will start with us and go the other way until you reach the first conveyer.

"Phase two. Kyle and Jessica will take care of their towers by placing some of the explosives we acquired on our raid of the compound on the legs here, here, and here." He pointed to three *corners* of the can representing the tower. "Yin and Sarah will do the same while I make my way through the empty gate, which we would have already taken out the guards stationed there, and I will disable the generator, setting an explosive in it to ensure the power doesn't come back on. If any N'Roth comes across you, try and take them out quietly, but if necessary, you can use your rifles or pistols.

"When I pull the power cells, it won't be long before someone comes to investigate, that's when I blow the explosives, and that's when phase three begins. Jessica, Yin, and I will begin making as much chaos as we can. We want the N'Roth to think there are twenty of us, which brings me to Sarah and Kyle. You two will have a few extra rifles and pistols on you. It's your job to get to the prison tents. As soon as your explosives are set, start heading that way. If Jessica

hasn't already shown you how to use the N'Roth explosives,

then get with her before we move out.

"Hopefully, you get there before I set them all off. If

not, that's okay. Start handing out your extra weapons and give

a crash course on how to use them. Tell the rest to grab

something they can use as a weapon and fight. If the N'Roth

get a call out for reinforcements, then we need to be ready to

retreat. We'll use those vehicles to escape. I've already talked

to Sarah and Jessica about disabling those arm trackers. The

only way to be sure that we disable them is to cut them out. We

can't come back here. We'll take the prisoners to that dried

riverbed that blocks the tracking signals. Once there, Sarah will

remove the trackers and use the healing device to close up the

wounds while the rest of us will take the transports and ditch

them. We'll all rendezvous back with Sarah and the prisoners.

Any questions, comments, additions, or suggestions?"

"Nope," Sarah replied.

"Good to go," Kyle said.

"I was able to set some of those radios to a secure channel so we can use them," Jessica added.

"Good," Aurik said. "That will make timing all this a whole lot easier. Do we have enough secure ones for each of us?"

Jessica nodded.

"Great, call signs are as follows. Sarah is Alpha two, Kyle, you are Bravo one, that makes Jessica Bravo two, Yin is Charlie one, and I am Alpha one."

The four each nodded as Aurik assigned their call signs.

"Kyle, Yin, you packed all of the explosives and weapons?" Aurik asked.

"Everything you told us," Kyle replied.

"Good. Sarah, I will carry that healing device because you will have those extra weapons stowed away in your pack."

Sarah nodded.

"If there isn't anything else, let's get our supplies and head out."

Minutes later, the squad was out of the cave and

heading for the prison camp.

277

22

When the squad reached the prison camp, they split into their teams, swiftly and quietly dispatching the N'Roth perimeter guards. Kyle and Sarah went about placing the explosives around their respective towers while Aurik, Jessica, and Yin made their way to their tactical placements.

Aurik reached the generator and waited for Kyle and Sarah to radio back that they had placed the explosive. Just a few moments later, Kyle's voice chirped over the radio that he had finished, then Sarah radioed in.

"Roger that, I'm pulling the power cells now," Aurik reported and yanked the cells from the generator, tossing them into his pack. With the removal of each power cell, the lights flickered; with the last cylinder, the prison camp went dark. After the last power cell was pulled, he placed one of the explosive canisters into the generator and retreated to the perimeter gate.

Just as he reached the gate, another transport emerged from the shadows of the forest, its blinding lights shining right on Aurik. He darted as fast as he could behind the edge of the ditch wall next to the gate, hoping he wasn't spotted.

"Bravo two, Alpha one. Are any transports missing, over?" Aurik whispered through his radio.

"That's a negative. All three transports are here, over," Jessica replied.

"Well, we have another transport at the gate. If anyone has a shot, take it now. I'm blowing the explosives, over." Aurik pulled the detonating device from his pocket and slid his finger across the digital pad, then pressed.

Instantaneously the darkness erupted in a series of blinding flashes, and ear-shattering booms as the bombs detonated. Then, the high pitched, gritty sound of metal bending filled the air as the two towers began to buckle under their own weight. With now only one functional supporting leg, the towers were unable to withstand their own weight, and they slowly tilted with loud, ear-piercing screeches until the leg finally gave out entirely, and the towers plummeted to the ground.

***

Sarah and Kyle reached the middle prisoner tent remarkably fast. Sarah was already kneeling in front of the tent as Kyle, gasping for air, reached her. She followed Kyle as he ducked through the flap of the tent.

The occupants were all already on their feet and mumbling about the sudden power outage by the time the two entered.

"Please!" Kyle hollered between heavy breaths as he slipped off his pack. "Listen up! We're here to set you free, listen up."

The occupants quieted down.

"Okay. Take a weapon. You will have to fight to be free of this enslavement! If you get an N'Roth rifle, step to the left. If you get a pistol, step to the right. We're going to show you how to use it. The rest of you, if you don't get a rifle or pistol, grab something, anything, you can use as a weapon."

Kyle and Sarah passed out the weapons and then instructed them on how to use them.

"You, you, and you," Kyle pointed to three men without guns. "You three go to the other tents and tell them to fight!" The three nodded.

Before he could send the three out of the tent, the explosives went off, sending everyone ducking to the floor except Sarah and Kyle, who flinched at the sudden assault to their senses.

"Are you ready?" Kyle yelled, "Get up! It's time to be free!" The prisoners stood and hollered. "Now, let's go!" Kyle ordered and led the charge out of the tent.

***

Yin found her way quickly down the cliffside, using one of the conveyor belts, and began firing at N'Roth soldiers fleeing from the crumbling towers. Shot after shot hit its mark, right in the chest of an enemy soldier.

She walked swiftly with her rifle up at the ready, looking down the muzzle, firing, then shifting and firing, then shifting and firing again. Each step took her closer to the falling tower until she was just a few paces from it as it slammed to the ground.

The panicked N'Roth who didn't meet their fate inside the fallen tower, and who managed to climb out of the rubble, finally found it at the blast of her rifle.

***

Aurik took advantage of the distracted N'Roth as they tried to make sense of the falling towers and sent a wave of rifle blasts into the soldiers before the aliens gained their composure and began firing back.

Aurik retreated into the shadows of the ditch, snatching up his pack on the way, then tossed a couple of grenade canisters behind him, then a couple into the center of the compound, before the remaining soldiers followed him into the darkness and to their demises.

***

Sarah and Kyle exited the tent and went straight for the towers. The prisoners split with them; the only exceptions were the three tasked with corralling the other tents into action and a handful who were charging at random N'Roth recovering from their falls.

Soon the other tents roared with the sound of revolution as the three sent to rally them fulfilled their tasks.

***

Jessica kept herself moving near the transports on the top of the cliff, eliminating any N'Roth unlucky enough to enter her visual range. On occasion, she tossed an N'Roth grenade canister, not necessarily intending to hit a specific target, but hoping to make it look like there were more than just the five of them attacking.

Aurik and Yin did the same, shooting and tossing canisters randomly, while Sarah and Kyle led their rebellion toward the two fallen towers.

When the tower closest to Jessica had finally crumbled, she began firing on those that climbed out of the wreckage. She picked them off, one by one, until a wave of the prisoners flooded the fallen tower, then she retreated to the three transports and waited, picking off any N'Roth which might have evaded death among the chaos blow.

***

Aurik slung his pack back over his shoulders, brought his rifle back up to his face, peering down the barrel, and began his tactical walk across the darkness of the ditch.

He found several targets that had somehow made it past the infuriated mob at the towers and dispatched them quickly with a smoldering blast to the chest, then tactically advanced deeper into the chaos of the battle.

***

Yin moved into the Shadow of the edge of the ditch and tossed a grenade cylinder into one of the large compartments of the fallen tower. Scratchy screams of the N'Roth fully realizing their fate erupted for just a few seconds, then were drowned out by the ensuing explosion.

She then inched her way along the cliff edge with her rifle up at the ready, sending an energy bolt toward anything that moved.

She saw a dozen N'Roth climbing out of a large compartment nearest the bottom of the tower and sent a wave of blasts into the compartment as she tactically marched nearer, her eye staring down the muzzle for quick aim. Some were greeted by an energy blast to the face, and others retreated back into their prison, narrowly dodging the ensuing energy blasts.

The wave of freed prisoners reached them, then jumping into the compartments and dispatching any surviving N'Roth.

***

Sarah and Kyle didn't have to do much as their small armies cleared every compartment, and every nook and cranny of the towers. The N'Roth, lucky enough to avoid the brutal death from the mob, found their ends at the rifle blasts from

Sarah or Kyle.

***

The battle was over swiftly, and Aurik ordered the

squad to begin loading the prisoners to the transports. Minutes

later, the prison camp was deserted.

Visit C. J. Korryn's website for more of his books.

https://www.cjkorryn.com/books

If you liked the book, read the monthly installments of season two and later seasons.

Connect with C. J. Korryn through: